Author's Foreword

This book is a work of historical fiction, though there are references to **Actual** persons in this book, and well as significant references to **Actual** events which have occurred throughout history this is in no way supposed to be a book on facts. So, though there will be some similarities to person's living or dead they are coincidental at best.

Now that I got the disclaimer out of the way. There have been many movies and books written since the time of H. G. Wells on time travel, and many theories have presented themselves within the course of the last two centuries. My inspiration behind this book was a thought, about; "what if someone actually messed up the timeline? What would be the consequences?" **Temporal Paradox Theory** is a curious theory which has existed for a long time behind the question of whether or not a person could exist if he went back in time and killed one of his predecessors. How would it be possible for him to do that? Would both parties therefore be erased from the timeline? And what would be the overreaching consequences of that action thereof?

In this writing I am going to challenge that very same question, however, I am not going to kill my main character to test the theory it would be ludicrous and would take away the very concept of the book. Rather, I am going to alter historical events, in such a manner that they could have dire effect on the future and then try to correct the problem before history is totally re-written.

There is an old saying "Those who don't remember history are doomed to repeat it." - George Santayana. Well, it is my hope that with writing this book and knowing that the events I am presenting will be based on facts and history, it is my hope that with this book, that you dear reader will have a better knowledge of history, and the consequences of messing around with it. Though it is oft said "History is written by the Victor."; the facts told within this novel will be those that are accepted as accurate on a world scale.

E.S.

A Time For Redemption

Prologue

Looking for redemption, Saul Millings was no stranger to taking multiple trips through the space-time continuum. He was 42 years old and a "Tempronaut", a term given to a new generation of soldiers trained in interdimensional time travel.

Why Saul was looking for redemption was simple. On one journey he violated the most sacred of rules given to any time traveler, and that was simply not to interfere with the timeline by changing history in any form.

Time soldiers have two jobs, their first and foremost were observers. They were to make sure that history followed in accordance with the recorded events, and second, they were to pursue any rogue time travelers whose sole purposes were to exploit time or smuggle temporal artifacts for other purposes.

Saul took his job very seriously.   He understood altering time could very well snuff out the existence of several prominent people on his own timeline. This included himself.

Of course, everyone has heard theories of temporal paradox. Basically, the meaning of which can be described in this brief statement. "If I went back in time and killed my grandfather, would I be alive in the present to have been able to do the same."

This paradox had troubled mankind for centuries. Long before the actual development of time travel vehicles and machines. The idea of time travel, alternate universes, or multi-verses, and the repercussions as well as rewards that could be gained would ever linger.

People for centuries were defining their own manifest destinies. Wondering is time linear? Are our lives predetermined? Do we control our destiny, or is it set in stone for us? All these questions would soon become revelations.

Saul Millings himself, was always fascinated by the concept. His great grandfather H. G. Wells had written of time travel and many of his writings predating modern technology had seemingly depicted the future. What many did not know however, until a stash of hidden papers was found carefully tucked away, was that Mr. Wells had actually succeeded in creating the first time machine, and his works which depicted some advanced technologies were actually factual and not fictional at all.

Chapter 1

From the Desk of: *Colonel Jack Spalding*

To: *Brigadier General Lancaster Thomas*

General Thomas, I received your letter concerning Professor Millings. Rest assured as soon as we can locate him in the timeline, we will make an all-out attempt to apprehend him.

However, I must remind you Sir that your patience in this matter will be greatly appreciated. I do realize that the longer it takes and the further he travels, the repercussions left in the wake can be irreversible.

It seems asking for patience in this matter seems to be an over-assuming undertaking, but due to Professor Milling's record and knowledge of history, I passionately believe that we will be able to catch him without much incidence.

Col. Jack Spalding, TTMCSXO

From the Desk of: *Brigadier General Lancaster Thomas*

To: *Colonel Jack Spalding.*

Lieutenant. I do not give a rat's ass how far you must go to get that renegade historian just bring that son of a bitch back here. Having him running around the S.T.C. is dangerous. He knows way too much, and our plans may be exposed. So, get him before he can get us.

Brig. Gen. Lance Thomas. ITCSCO

From the Desk of: *Colonel Jack Spalding*

To: *Brigadier General Lancaster Thomas*

Sir you referred to me as Lieutenant, was that in error?

Colonel Jack Spalding

From the Desk of: *Brigadier General Lancaster Thomas*

To: *Colonel Jack Spalding*

If you do not get him soon, you will soon find out whether I said that in error, or if I was serious.

Brigadier General Lance Thomas.

Colonel Spalding was now concerned. The

telex that came across his com desk made it perfectly clear that his career and his goals of becoming a full bird Colonel would not happen unless he apprehended Saul Millings. But therein lies the rub.

Saul was the best at his job, ,he was a historian, a scholar, a soldier, and most importantly a scientist like his great grandfather. He was perhaps the best tracker the ITC had on staff. So, for Colonel Spalding to find him, more or less, and apprehend him, was indeed a daunting task.

Chapter 2

Saul had originally found the documents. However, he was unable to keep them hidden long. The Department of National Security had Saul under investigation for a while. The reason for all the surveillance was because Saul was a Professor of History at Stanford University. He had several degrees and was also known to be a collector of historical artifacts. So, when Saul discovered his grandfather's papers, the DNS swooped in and confiscated them.

Having discovered that the documents contained plans for the actual building and creating of a time traveling device (i.e., Time Machine), the plans were then turned over to a specialized research department run by the United States Military.

It took the department 2 months to analyze the documents and construct the second time machine ever built. (The first was actually built by H.G. Wells). After 8 years of continual testing, they finally determined that it was safe for humans to operate. And now they needed to find the right candidates for the job of their first test pilot.

Many candidates from all branches of the Armed Services stepped up to try to get the job as the first person to travel in time, but due to psychological profiles, historical knowledge, and various other mitigating circumstances finding the ideal candidate was a daunting endeavor.

Until Brigadier General Lancaster Thomas, Head of the Science and Research Division of the United States Air Force, reached out to Director Martin Oberman, head of the DNS and asked him where they had obtained the papers.

From the Desk of: *Brigadier General Lancaster Thomas (COUSAF-SRD)*

To: *NSD Director Martin Oberman*

Martin as you are well aware since the discovery of the documents, and H. G. Well's letters we have been diligently working on the recreation of specific portions of the documents you discovered. We have successfully managed to reproduce one of the many different items listed in the documents. However, I am not at liberty to divulge which item it is at current due to the top-secret nature of our program and projects.

I am sure given your initial analysis of the documents, and your intelligence, you can probably ascertain which of those many items listed in the letters we have been working on, and which we have currently achieved.

Here, however is where we have reached a conundrum of a sort. We are unable to find the proper candidate to initiate our testing of said item. Do you have someone, perhaps that you have a full dossier on that you feel may be the ideal candidate, and do you have access to him/her to actually be able to recruit same individual? If so, kindly please reach out to him/her and send said individual to my office at the Pentagon.

Brigadier General Lance Thomas COUSAF-SRD

From the Desk of: N.S.D. Director Martin Oberman

To: Brigadier General Lancaster Thomas (COUSAF-SRD)

As a matter of fact, Sir, We do have a

candidate that would be perfect as the first test pilot for said device. And, Yes, I am pretty much able to ascertain, what device it is. Therefore, I am sending you the dossier of Professor Saul Millings. His dossier should speak for itself. In addition, he is also the founder of the letters which you have in your possession, so it would behoove us to keep him under our command, so that we can maintain control of the situation.

NSD Director Martin Oberman

Two weeks later, Saul received a letter in the mail. He almost did not open the letter as soon as he saw it was addressed from the National Security Department. You see, Saul had spent all his life, since he was around 14 years old collecting historical artifacts. His father Jacob had got him started on his path when they went to the museum, where his father Jacob was the curator. While his father would be busy cataloguing new additions and donations to the museum, Saul would wander around and read all the descriptions on them.

Never totally satisfied, Saul would often see an artifact that caught his eye and go to the museum records and library and start heavily researching the history of the item. During his high school years, Saul would often be seen with his nose in some history book or in the school library doing research on a various decade in history. Not much for having a social life, people tended to believe he was eccentric. Saul on the other hand was not eccentric, but he was obsessed.

This obsession with history would eventually lead to Saul going to college and pursuing his dream of becoming an historian, and an archeologist. After 12 years of college, he earned his Ph.D. in History and a second Ph. D. in Ethnology, A Master's Degree in Archeology, and a master's degree in Anthropology. Upon graduating from Stanford University, he soon became Professor Emeritus and head of the Historical Studies Department of Stanford.

Through his obsessive fascination with history, Saul began to devote some of his time and energy into researching his own genealogical background. It was in this research that he discovered that he was the great-grandson of none other than H.G. Wells. At the age of 30 he began to collect every work ever written by his great grandfather. It was in reading his grandfather's book, The Time Machine, that Saul's curiosity really peaked.

There was a strange correlation between his grand-father's seemingly fictional work of the day, and the advances in modern society. Was, his grandfather a psychic? Did his grandfather actually predict the future? Or did we start developing the technologies based off of his grandfather's strange and fascinating ideas? These questions plagued Saul.

So, when Saul got the letter, still intently annoyed with the fact that he had found letters from his grandfather and was not able to sit down with them, due to the fact that they were confiscated by the NSD that he was hesitant to open the letter. Saul set the letter on his desk, poured a scotch, and decided to prepare his next lecture. Forgetting the letter was even on his desk, Saul went about his standard day for the next two to three weeks.

While preparing a lecture on the development of the legal systems of society from

Prehistory to the Modern Age, he suddenly remembered that he had received a letter from the NSD. He decided then to open the letter. With a little hesitation he began to read the letter expecting the worse from it. Instead, however, he was to be pleasantly surprised.

To the Desk of: *Saul Millings, Professor Emeritus, History Department, Stanford University*

From: *NSD Director Martin Oberman*

Professor Millings, I realize that you probably are rather disconcerted about our removing from your possession the series of documents written by H. G. Wells, that you discovered. We, for reasons of National Security, thought it would be better if we had possession of them, due to the nature of the content of those letters. I am sure you are aware that if the public were to get ahold of such material, that there could have been dire consequences, not only for the security of our nation, but also to the security of the world as we know it.

"What the hell is he talking about?" Saul thought to himself. Of course, Saul was unable to even begin to research the letters for content before they were abruptly removed, so as far as he knew they could have been love letters to his grandmother.

That being said, we are now willing to let you have access to these letters, your knowledge of History, and being that you found these, very intriguing documents, requires us to call upon you to provide a beneficial service to your country and potentially the world.

"Service? What the Hell is this guy talking about?" "What the hell was in those letters?"

If you would be willing to indulge a few minutes of your time, we would like you to report to the Pentagon. Please request to see Brigadier General Lancaster Thomas. He is expecting you. He will explain everything when you get there.

Martin Oberman, Director NSD.

"The Pentagon? What the hell is the military doing with those documents?" Now totally intrigued Saul had no choice. He had to find out what was in those letters, and he also wanted to get them back. They in all truth, belonged to him. Not only by the fact that he found them, but also by default because they were from a family member.

Chapter 3

The very next day, Saul booked a train to Washington, D.C. He knew it would take him 3 days by rail to get there, and he wanted to take the time necessary to re-read the letter. You see, to Saul, nothing was ever as simple as it appeared to be. The letter said to report to the Pentagon rather than the National Security Department Headquarters in Virginia. So, Saul was wondering what the military had to do with his grandfather's letters or why they have them in the first place. Yes, H.G. Wells was an especially important man, his writings stirred a lot of controversy. Little did Saul realize, however, that these letters had increased his importance a thousand-fold. "What weren't they telling him?" "Why all the secrets behind these letters? "And, Why are they in the Pentagon?" All these questions continued to haunt Saul.

H.G. Wells born 1866 died 1946(?) was a prominent fiction writer. In the course of 12 years, he wrote as many as 13 books, an average of a book a year. Many of his books were acclimated toward social conditions at the time and contained descriptions of sociological and economic conditions within the United Kingdom. However, behind these stories, there was an autobiographical concealment, which to the untrained and unaware reader would not be able to ascertain.

So, his most famous work, *The Time Machine*, published in 1895, which had begun as a short story he had written for his college magazine called *"The Chronic Argonauts"* (1888) became a novel of curiosity, and a driving point behind Saul's peaked curiosity, as well as the reason Saul would be called to appear before the military.

To the many persons who read the novel this was a work of science fiction and fantasy, there was no possible way that Mr. Well's Traveler could have possibly built a machine to travel through time nor had actually the capability of achieving it. For all intent and purpose, though, the unending desire was always in the forefront, the ability to traverse the fourth dimension (time) would be impossible.

In the 1930's all the way to the 1980's many people in many different colleges and research and development organizations, both public and private have devised multiple experimental methodologies in order to transcend that seemingly obscure dimension. Many based their theories on the mathematical formulae of Dr. Albert Einstein (and his Theory of Relativity). Having already been capable of splitting the atom and creating the first atomic weapons in 1945 and releasing them over Hiroshima and Nagasaki, thus giving birth to the Atomic Revolution. Of course, the next logical step would be "experimenting with time itself".

We had already broken the speed of sound, we were familiar with the speed of light, we had awareness of the vastness of space and many theories and postulates were in play as for the origin of the species, and the universe. Everything from the Big Bang to the Oscillating Universe Theory were already conceptualized, so of course the next logical step which we would discover occurred millennia ago, was to transverse time itself.

Chapter 4

Saul arrived in Washington D.C. on March 27, 2028, at 1500. He checked into the Hilton Garden Inn and took a well needed shower. While in the shower he replayed the letter from Oberman in his head. His curiosity, still peaking a great deal. "What was in those letters?" "Why were they so important?" They assumed I had already had the opportunity of reading them. So obviously, there is something in them that must have a very profound or detrimental meaning to what they consider the nation's security.

Saul stepped out of the shower, poured himself a scotch and turned on the television. However, he was still so engrossed in thought regarding the letter that he didn't even pay attention to what was being broadcasted on the news.

Four hours later, a supposition finally struck him. All this time from childhood he wondered if his grandfather had actually built a machine capable of time travel, and whether it was even possible.

Because of the mysterious content of the letter, and of course, the immediate concern of the military and the Pentagon, he realized that it was possible that his grandfather had actually built the machine, and that the letters may have contained the plans for the construction of same. It only made sense that the government probably made a copy of the machine and it worked.

Saul went to bed. He woke the following morning, took a shower, rented a car, and headed to the Pentagon. On his way to the Pentagon, Saul decided to take a detour. He decided that he would make a quick stop at the Smithsonian Museum to try to clear his head. Saul had always wanted to go to the Smithsonian, because it was claimed to hold the biggest archive of history that existed in the United States. Plus, it would give him an opportunity to assess the situation and reason for this trip. Saul was trying to convince himself to change his mind about responding to the letter.

Across town at the Chronological Research Center. A secret facility located 10 stories below the Pentagon, a final test run and experiment with the new time machine was about to commence.

General Thomas was seated in the observation deck, watching the technicians work on the final settings of the machine. They set the clock forwards approximately 20 minutes and prepared to fire up the device. A countdown commenced, and the technicians left the vicinity to ensure their safety. Unaware of what the results might be they didn't want to be in the same room as the machine when it started up.

The last three minutes of the countdown seemed to take forever, all the stats and dials looked correct and there didn't seem to be any complications. In the last ten seconds everyone present looked on in anticipation. Carefully observing through the light tempering glass. 5—4—3—2—1 a blinding flash of light and suddenly the machine had vanished. A timer was now set in the control room for 20 minutes anticipating whether the machine would suddenly reappear.

Meanwhile, at the same time the experiment is commencing, Saul is in the museum looking over a few artifacts. He suddenly felt an odd sensation as if a wave of energy was just released, like a small earthquake. The item he was looking at, the Purple Heart belonging to Audie Murphy, suddenly vanished. Saul did a double-take and the purple heart reappeared but upside down in the case. "Curious" thought Saul, "I could have sworn it was in an upright position." "Ahhh! Whatever! The person who put it in there probably just laid it in there without paying attention." Saul dismissed the sudden distraction as just random chance.

Unbeknownst to him it was anything but random. One of the side effects of temporal travel was sudden fluxes in the space time continuum. And small simple objects that have history often are affected.

In the interim, across town, at a jeweler's shop, all the clocks suddenly jumped forward 20 seconds. It was barely noticeable to the jeweler, and he would not have noticed, had it not been for the wind spring on the one he was working on suddenly tensed up by itself before giving a quick release and shooting across the room.

"Dammit" "Something is seriously wrong with this

watch." "Now I have to replace the whole damn works."

Back at the laboratory 19 minutes later, another countdown commenced.

Nervously anticipating what was going to happen in the next minute. General Thomas wiped his brow. There was a sudden vibration, a slight bang, and the Time Machine appeared out of thin air right where it had disappeared from. Success! Holy Shit! Time travel can be achieved! H.G. was right!

Chapter 5

March 29, 1627, in the small French settlement on the Isle of Tortuga off the coast of Haiti. An unassuming gentleman in a long coat, brown trousers, a white ruffled shirt, with medium length brownish-grey hair, and a grey beard, sat in an inn. This gentleman appeared to be approximately 60 years of age. He was drinking a tankard of Jamaican rum and smoking a pipe.

While beginning to sip his rum, Armand felt a slight disturbance around him. No one else seemed to notice but there was a slight tremor and a sudden pulse of energy which seemed to pass right through him. Armand nonchalantly moved his shirt sleeve slightly up his arm, exposing very briefly the wristwatch he was wearing. He quickly noticed that the second hand on the watch was suddenly travelling backwards.

He stood up from his chair quickly covered his watch with his jacket sleeve, left a gold doubloon on the table and stepped out of the inn into the alleyway. Surveying his surroundings for any passers-by , he looked again at his watch, the second hand was still travelling in reverse. Armand had only seen this happen once before and that was when he actually began testing the Time Machine that he had built. "This can't be happening again. I haven't generated the infernal machine since I hid it here in Tortuga". Somehow, somewhere, somewhen, someone had developed another time travelling device, and this caused Armand a great deal of disconcertion, because indeed if someone had created another machine, their interference could disrupt the entire space time continuum. Especially if they didn't know exactly what they were getting into or what they were doing.

Armand quickly returned to where he left his machine, and immediately proceeded to get into it. He asked himself "when and where do I set the dials?" For twenty minutes he sat there pondering the question and suddenly looked again at his watch. The wristwatch returned to normal.

Well to Armand this was good news and bad news. The good news was they haven't perfected it yet therefore, he has time to figure out the when and where, and the bad news was that he knows they are on the verge of a breakthrough, and if he doesn't find out soon, they may indeed succeed.

Then the next thing occurred to him, "If they do succeed, will they come looking for me?" "And if so, have they developed the technology to track my movements through time and space.?"

General Thomas went upstairs to his office. After experiencing the successful run of the experiment, he was still left with loads of questions. Yes, they set everything to basically have the machine return to the same location 20 minutes in the future, yes it seemingly worked. But still, what would be the adverse effects of the machine on the human body?

General Thomas called in one of the technicians. "We can't possibly test this on a human being just yet. We don't know if there are any adverse effects. Is there a way we can test this on several different medias to see how it affects each.?"

The technician replied. "Yes, Sir!" "We can test it on a few animals and measure them before and after for any effects. We can observe them physically and psychologically to predict changes in their behaviors. As well as search for physical deformities."

"Well, let's just do that. I cannot risk taking a chance that we may accidently damage or kill someone without first knowing whether or not this phenomenon will have any adverse effects." "Do you remember the Philadelphia Experiment?" "No Sir! I do not." "Well according to the documents filed after the experiment they found bodies melted into various parts of the ship. People still living but were completely melded with the ship." "That's horrifying." "Indeed." "And we really don't need another incident like that occurring that we have to cover up."

Saul arrived at the Pentagon. He pulled up to the gate. The guard at the gate stopped him and asked his business. Saul stated, "I am here to see General Lancaster Thomas." The guard took his name, told him to wait right there and walked into his booth to call in.

The Guard came out of the booth and handed Saul a visitors pass. "The General is expecting you." "You will find his office on the 3rd floor wing 3 room 33. " Saul of course found this interesting that all the numbers would be corresponding, but said nothing but "Thank You"

Saul parked his rental in a designated area and proceeded to the main entrance. He was met there by another guard who checked his pass. To his astonishment entering the Pentagon was like entering a small city. It had all sorts of stores, amenities, restaurants, and offices built into the same building. Saul reminded himself that after the meeting with the General that he would take advantage of his pass and explore this very historic building.

Chapter 6

Saul walked over to section 3 admiring the sights as he went. There were a lot of things to see within the Pentagon, but he didn't have time to take all of them in.

He passed the guard stations at each sector, emptied his pockets, and proceeded to the elevator. Another strange sensation passed through Saul. As he entered the elevator. It was like he had been here before. But he couldn't recall when. He marked it off as a case of déjà vu.

Saul was never one to take heed of those various synchronicities that were occurring in his life. He always believed in coincidence and whenever something unusual or bizarre occurred he normally just wrote it off. However, As of late he had been noticing more and more random coincidences and events, and they were beginning to become not so random at all. Saul was thinking about this matter. "Why suddenly are these strange things cropping up around me?" "Ah, It must be nerves is all." And Saul continued up to the third floor.

He entered the office 33 at 3:33 pm.

"Again, all those threes." He was greeted at the desk by an attractive 5' 6" blonde-haired, blue-eyed AFC, "I'm here to see General Thomas." "Your Name." "Saul Millings" "One moment please."

She punched the name in on her com desk and then forwarded a fast message to General Thomas. "Sir, there is a Saul Millings to see you". "Send him in". "The General is expecting you." "Do I salute or something?" "No, you're a civilian."

Saul entered the office. He quickly surveyed his surroundings. "Have a seat Mister Millings." "I'd prefer to stand if you don't mind, I don't expect to be here long." "I SAID SIT DOWN!" Saul sat down. There was something in the General's voice that said that this meeting might take a while. "The General raised his com desk and told the secretary to bring in the dossier on Saul Millings.

"Mister Millings, I assume you know why you are here." "Actually, I don't" "All I know is that is has something to do with the letters that I found that apparently wound up in your possession." "That is precisely why you are here." "Do you know the contents of those letters?" "No actually I don't.

I wasn't able to peruse them before they were confiscated by the NSD."

"Okay well let's get down to brass tacks then." "The letters you found contained some very interesting content." "What sort of content?", inquired Saul. "It says here you are a collector of H.G. Wells' works." "Are you aware that Mr. Wells was not only a writer, but also an inventor of sorts.?" "Well, I assumed he was some sort of scientist, because a lot of the material in his works just didn't add up to the technologies of the time, he wrote them." "He was indeed a scientist and inventor. These letters actually hold in them several plans for many of his inventions." "But what has that got to do with me?" "Well, it says here you're a historian " "Are you familiar with the story he wrote called *"The Chronic Argonauts"?"* "Yeah, it was a short story he was developing while writing for his college newspaper concerning time travel. It was an excellent work of fiction."

"Well, what if I was to tell you it wasn't fictional at all?" Saul did a double take. "It wasn't a work of fiction?" "As a matter of fact, no. You see we discovered in these letters the actual plans and blueprints to build a time machine." "But time travel is impossible." "Is it though?" "Everything we've ever studied indicates that time is not a measurable dimension." "Our research and development department has determined that Mister Wells, had indeed proven otherwise. After careful analysis of these papers, and after multiple formulations and calculations, we determined that not only was time travel possible, but Mister Wells actually built a time machine." "What?" "Precisely our first reaction as well." "Anyway, utilizing these letters, we were able to duplicate several of Mister Wells' experiments and we have recreated the very time machine that he designed and potentially constructed. Though we are not entirely sure that he succeeded." "We have run several tests however, and recent conclusions are that this contraption actually functions and is in fact a genuine time travelling device." Saul stood up, "I'm leaving I don't think I want to hear any more of this conversation." "SIT BACK DOWN, WE ARE NOT FINISHED YET!"

Hesitantly, Saul sat back down. All the while so many questions and thoughts were running through his head. "All this while the time machine actually exists at least in theory. Can my grandfather have really created this machine? If so, is he actually not dead, but is travelling throughout time?" "If he is, then, Is there a chance that everything we have known about him has been a lie?"

Chapter 7

Armand (aka H.G. Wells) set his time machine forward to 1895. He realized that if he returned to his own time period he could hide in plain sight. Because he knew all the places that he would visit regularly he also could avoid running into himself on the timeline. Thus, not disturbing the course of events. However, one thought did occur to him, "what if I didn't create that infernal machine to begin with?" "If I could prevent myself from creating it, I could alter history and thus not have to run around the centuries hiding anymore. "

H.G. had come to the realization a long time ago, however, that changing the course of history could have dire consequences. Therefore, knowing that fact, he also knew that he had to let history run its proper course. Recently there were several events however, that were causing him a great deal of concern. Being he had traveled frequently through time he also became aware of events and fluctuations that began to occur whenever he operated his time machine. Certain experiences and feelings indicated the various shifts in the timeline, to which he began paying very close attention.

Normally these would occur only when he was operating his own machine. But they were suddenly occurring despite the fact that he wasn't travelling. This could only lead to one conclusion. On some other timeline, someone had recreated his invention and was actually using it. This could prove to be detrimental not only to his future but to the past as well. Especially if the person's utilizing the machine hadn't a full grasp of history.

A very interesting occurrence happened when he arrived in his own timeline. He stepped out of the machine, and it disappeared. Apparently objects of the exact same type cannot occupy the same space at the same time. Which means he would need to find his original time machine in order to travel again. Of course, he knew where to find it, if indeed it didn't disappear. It would be in the basement of his house. But another problem arose to him. What if both machines went out of existence, That would mean, that he himself on this timeline would also know something was amiss. He would have to be extra diligent in avoiding himself.

In the meantime, in the basement of 141 Mayberry Road, Woking, H.G. Wells was working on his time machine. While building it he was trying to adjust the chronograph and suddenly it fell out of existence. "Strange!" he thought. I didn't set the chronograph, yet the machine vanished.

This very event piqued his curiosity. Something definitely wasn't correct, and the machine should not have activated itself, if indeed it did. He retired to his study to go over his notes and his blueprints. He was totally unaware of the events that had occurred and felt as if the machine was just activated by sheer accident.

The machine wasn't activated as he was later to discover. It had indeed dematerialized due to the very nature of time itself being interrupted by a concurrent event, which originated in the future.

H. G. Wells wasn't sure whether to write off the machine's sudden disappearance as a success or a failure. On one hand the machine may have incidentally slipped into the time stream and may be headed for its destination, on the other hand a strange phenomenon, (which proved to be the latter) had caused the machine to simply be snuffed out of existence.

H.G. decided that his next course of action once arriving was to go to the local pub for a drink. He knew he wasn't destined to arrive there any time soon because of the fact that his other self would be in his study working up until around 7:30 pm , and that he would soon retire to sleep afterwards.

One of the advantages in being a time traveler was in the knowing of what events had already occurred or in his case would be occurring as he knew well his alternate self. "Avoiding myself should be relatively easy.", he thought to himself. As long as I change destinations as to where I normally went, I should be fine.

His surroundings were very familiar to him. He had and was residing in this location and timeline for many years. Much to his chagrin, however, he was to find that after this current chain of accidental events, his other self would change his routine. Not anticipating this potential change H.G proceeded to attempt to live out his life in hiding in plain sight.

Chapter 8

"What do you want from me?", inquired Saul. "Mister Millings we are well aware that you are the great-grandson of Mister Wells, and that you have been a collector of his works for some time." "How long have I been under surveillance?" "That is not for me to answer." "But because we you have discovered these most important letters; we have decided that we would like you to be the one to actually test the time machine." "However, we're not going to have you test it yet. Not until we determine whether there are any adverse effects resultant from time travel." "That's very considerate of you.", said Saul sarcastically.

"We are going to run several more test in the course of this month to determine the machines effects." General Thomas continued. "Once they are complete would you be willing to become our first traveler?" Saul said, "Would you allow me the courtesy to at least think about this awhile before I actually agree to become your guinea pig?" "Certainly. We wouldn't want you to just jump into a decision like this without first allowing you to make up your own mind."

Saul stood up and, "With your permission General may I be excused ?" "Yes! You may go. Come back to us in about a month from now, with your decision."

Saul left the general's office. Now totally distracted he no longer was interested in browsing around the Pentagon. Saul just wanted to get back to the hotel, grab a stiff drink and think about all that transpired. Another strange sensation came upon him. After considering the day's events, Saul concluded that the sensations he was experiencing recently were the results of them running tests on the time machine. Now knowing firsthand, that indeed the machine existed, he started to recognize that all these strange occurrences that kept happening around him were the result of the testing of the machine. "But why am I effected by it, and not everyone else?"

Unbeknownst to Saul these effects were not only occurring to him. They were being felt and seen now and then by others but being written off, much like he was originally writing them off himself.

Saul took the train back to Stanford. Upon arriving at his residence, he was too tired to even think about the events that had transpired. Not even taking off his clothes or shoes he went right to bed. Saul fell asleep while thinking about the day and began having dreams about the meeting with the general.

In his dream he was trying to figure out exactly what the general wanted him to do. "Would he just be a test pilot or was there going to be more too it?" Saul dreamt that he was on a military installation going through an intense program of basic training. After he completed the training, he was in an AIT school where he was instructed on the practices of time travel, history, and law. Little did Saul realize this dream of his was precognitive. He would indeed be going through those exact same courses in a few months' time.

Due to the fact that the military made the time machine and in addition copied all the letters Saul had found, the General agreed to return the originals to Saul. Saul of course had locked them up in what he considered a very safe place, and for the next few months he went about his normal business working at the University, giving lectures, attending meetings, grading papers and so forth.

Three months went by relatively quickly and Saul received a letter from General Thomas.

From the Desk of: *General Lancaster Thomas (COUSAF-SRD)*

To: *Professor Saul Millings, Professor Emeritus, Head of Stanford University History Department.*

Professor Millings. I am assuming that I have given you enough time to think about our proposal. We have done in the last three months extensive research on living and non-living things utilizing the time machine and have determined that it would be safe to send a person through the continuum without causing any severe adverse effects on that individual.

We again have taken all points into consideration, and we have considered you our best candidate for the initial actual run of the time machine. We will take all preventative and safety measures necessary to provide for your personal safety and will be able to perform the initial interaction relatively risk free.

We hope that you have considered our proposal and that you'd be willing to undertake this adventure.

Sincerely and with greatest regards, General Lancaster Thomas (COUSAF-SRD)

Chapter 9

Tuesday, May 15, 2018, after 5 months surveillance on a building in Kandahar, Afghanistan Abigail Thorn, had finally got her man. Abu Al-Hazreed. She saw him enter the building on several occasions and decided it was high time to report her findings to JSOC.

There was a capture or kill order on Al-Hazreed due to the fact that he was a Taliban leader who had connections with Al Qaeda as well as ISIS and he was responsible for several of the terrorist attacks on the civilian population of Afghanistan as well as also some of the Military installations.

Little did she realize however that the building itself was a civilian hospital and Al-Hazreed was visiting his young nephew aged 14 who had suffered an injury during one of the many actions that occurred. She basically assumed it was an Isis stronghold and decided this was the best time to actually catch or kill Al-Hazreed.

She took a MAC flight out of Kandahar International Airport which at the time was being used as an Airbase for the US Military. She arrived at

Ft. Bragg on May 15th. She reported her findings to Lieutenant Colonel Lancaster Thomas who was in charge at the time of the new JSOC Drone Operations Unit.

Lieutenant Colonel Thomas called her into his office. "So, Agent Thorn, I was told you were catching an early flight out of Kandahar, have you found one of our targets?" "As a matter of fact, Colonel yes I have and you're going to be happy to know that I believe I've also found one of the many strongholds held by the Taliban." "Well, we can probably take out another building with a regular airstrike. However, that's not going to stop the Taliban from just occupying another location." "Have you got anything else for me?" "Your email said that you had some very important information for me concerning a high-profile target who is it?"

"Well, we have established surveillance on Al –Hazreed, and we have seen him enter this particular building at least 6 times a month. We feel strongly that this is an Al Qaeda stronghold, and we know his routine enough to pinpoint an exact date and time he will be entering it. "

"He will most likely return to the building on May 17th, He normally stays inside approximately 15 to 35 minutes so our window will be extremely limited. So, if we're going to act on this it'll have to be soon. We will maintain surveillance and should be ready for him when he arrives at the building".

"We have a capture or kill order on Al-Hazreed what would be the CIA's recommendation?" "I'd say two Blackhawks, SEAL 9 and we go for a capture. The CIA is very interested in what intelligence we can gain from Al-Hazreed" "So you're recommending a capture?" "It would be preferable but would also be a high-risk operation due to the fact that this building itself is in a highly travelled civilian area." And we wouldn't be able to do a night raid, because of the fact he normally arrives there at midafternoon"

"Well Abby I only have one thing to say. It looks as if a capture might not be possible." "With such a short window of opportunity we'd be better off with a drone strike." "What if there are civilians in the building?" "Collateral damage, it happens in war, and we cannot determine directly who are armed combatants of who are civilians in this instance. Therefore, it would be best to assume they are all armed combatants, and we take the building out as a military target." "If indeed this operation goes south for any reason, I will take full responsibility for it and will leave the CIA out of it." "It's your call Colonel."

"I will be in contact with our surveillance team, and we will inform you when the operation is a go." Abigail was quite sure that she had all the information correct. She and her team had been following Al-Hazreed for several months looking for the right opportunity. However, she would have preferred it was a capture operation rather than a kill op. Because she wanted vital intelligence on some of the other Leaders.

Due to the opportunity however to finally get her mark, she knew that a kill op was going to have to be the only option. She contacted her team in Kandahar and let them know what was going to occur. She also warned them to not be in the area as it was determined to be a kill op and she didn't want her team in the crossfire.

Chapter 10

Lieutenant Colonel Thomas was on the fast track to a promotion. He knew that if this mission turned out to be a success, he would become a full bird colonel and be able to run his own command instead of just a single unit within JSOC. So, he immediately went to the command center and called the White House Situation Room.

He ran the information he received about Al-Hazreed to the Joint Chiefs, the Secretary General and the President. Informing them of the intelligence gathered and the scope of the operation and awaited approval. Because Al-Hazreed was a high profile target the members of the situation room and the president all agreed to proceed with the operation, and they authorized the use of a drone strike.

So, it was then scheduled. The next sighting of Al-Hazreed entering the building would be the day the operation commenced. It was two days later when Abby receives the intelligence that he was inside the building that they commenced with the operation.

Lieutenant Colonel Thomas then commanded Captain Spalding who happened to be the drone pilot on duty to take control of the drone, the target had entered the building and from across the street Abby's team was observing the whole building filming it as well as painting it with an infrared device. When they were assured that Al-Hazreed was in the building they put down the marker and set the target. It took the predator approximately 17 minutes to reach the building and light it up.

Little did they realize until after the damage was done that the building was a civilian hospital, 35 civilian and non-combatant casualties occurred many of them women and children. The focus was so intent on getting Al-Hazreed that they didn't do their due diligence. The CIA had botched the operation and so did JSOC.

Of course, so as not to look bad or anything, there was a massive coverup which extended all the way to the White House. The back story was it was a gas-line explosion which occurred in the hospital basement which resulted in the ignition of oxygen tanks which caused the major explosion within the building itself.

The actual truth about the incident was hidden and the Lieutenant Colonel was promoted to Colonel and given his own command outside of JSOC to buy his silence. Meanwhile Abby too was promoted for fostering the mission to take out Al-Hazreed and she became Senior Agent for her team.

Captain Spalding was also promoted as well to Major. So needless to say, a lot of silence was bought and paid for. This was the secret that was referred to in the correspondence between General Thomas and Colonel Spalding that needed to be kept that way.

If it were to come out into the open, there would be a lot of heads including the President's which would roll in the White House. So, promotions were given, commands changed, and silence bought, and all things considered the world returned to normal for those involved. Except it really didn't return to normal. Another chain of events would occur that would revitalize the situation and potentially lead to an investigation which would not have been good for any involved.

So, keeping this whole affair under wraps was of vital importance.

Chapter 11.

Three months later Saul was on his way back to the Pentagon. He had indeed seriously considered the General's proposal. If there was one thing that drove Saul more than anything it was History. So, what better opportunity could present itself than for him to actually go back into time itself and experience history firsthand instead of just reading about it in books or studying artifacts. What if he could actually travel through time itself and be able to understand history from the perspective of those who lived it?

Saul took the three-day trip with great anticipation. He knew that he was preparing for the adventure of his lifetime. But a lot of questions started coming into his mind. "How would time travel affect him personally?" "Would he perpetually stay the same age?" "Would travelling backwards through time cause him to become younger rather than older?" "What would happen if he should run into himself, or another aspect of himself?" "What if he ran into one of his own ancestors, like his great-grandfather?" How would it affect his current timeline?" "Would it alter history for him and possibly others?"

Saul arrived in Chicago. He had a 4-hour layover, so he figured he'd sit at the restaurant in the station grab a quick bite to eat and relax for a few. Across from his table sat a lady around the same age as him and she was eating her lunch and relaxing. Saul paid little heed because he was still engrossed in his inner dialogue. Two Middle Eastern gentlemen sitting at another table in front of his suddenly began talking in Farsi.

Saul being a linguist could understand their conversation. Soon the topic jumped to American Women and their thoughts on how all women should behave.

"min ghayr almunasib tmaman 'an tajlis alnisa' fi al'amakin aleamat wawujuhuhuna makshufatan. 'iinaha bihajat 'iilaa airtida' alhijab wahal yumkinuk 'an taraa eulbat alsajayir tilk fi jaybiha muqazizatan waghayr qanuniatin."

{It's totally inappropriate for women to be sitting in public with their faces exposed. She needs to wear a hijab and can you see that pack of cigarrettes in her pocket that's disgusting and unlawful.)

Saul immediately, after hearing that part of their conversation spoke out.

"limadha la tahtamu bishuuwnik alkhasati. hadhih 'amrika , lidha 'iidha kunt la tuhibu qawaeidana 'aw 'uslub hayatina , farjie min hayth 'ataytu."

(Why don't you mind your own business. This is America, so if you don't like our rules or way of life go back where you came from.)

A slight blush came across the face of the young woman. She smiled and began giggling.

She turned to face Saul and mouthed the word. *"Batali" (My Hero).*

Saul invites her to come join him at his table. "Hi Im Saul and you are?" "I'm Abby pleased to meet you Saul" "Thank you for coming to my defense, however unnecessary that it was." "I understood exactly what they said just chose to ignore it." "You're welcome. I didn't know you spoke Farsi." "It's not a common language to understand." "Well, Saul, you also speak it well. Have you ever been to the Middle East.?" "Actually,

I have not." "Well, you speak it almost as good as a native." "What do you do as an occupation?" "I'm a historian, and a professor of History at Stanford." "You understood what they were saying?" "Yes." "Well how did you learn Farsi?" "I grew up in the Middle East my adoptive parents worked at the embassy in Cairo."

So, Saul and Abby spent the next 4 hours enjoying each other's company. They both realized they were both linguists and began conversing in multiple foreign languages and comparing notes.

Time at that point seemed to melt away. And both of them soon realized it was time to board their respective trains.

"So, Abby where are you headed?" "I'm headed to D.C." "What a coincidence I'm headed to D.C. as well, would you like to spend the rest of the trip in my company? I would really enjoy having a travelling companion" "Certainly" Abby reached in her purse for her wallet about ready to pay for both their lunches. "This one's on me Abby." Saul called the waitress over and paid for their lunches. "Such a gentleman." Abby laughed.

Chapter 12

AIC Abigail Thorn was called into her Directors office.

After the successful kill mission on Al-Hazreed though it was not without cost Abigail was promoted to Agent In Charge (AIC) and moved into the Chicago field office. She missed the excitement of being out in the field and being part of a field team. Instead, she was stuck at a menial desk job training new agent recruit and basically analyzing incoming data from the fields worldwide. What she wouldn't do for a HALO jump into hostile territory. She loved the adrenaline. It was what drove her. So, when the director called her into his office, she was sincerely hoping this was a chance for her to get back in the field.

"What is it Sir?" "Please tell me it's a field op. I want to go back out into the shit." "Actually, Abby I believe this assignment is right up your alley." The Director hands her an envelope with EYES ONLY stamped on it. It was entirely sealed and unopened. "Sir, are you sure this is for me?"

":It came directly from Virginia to the farm,

and it was addressed to you strictly." "Hell, I'm not even aware of what's in it."

"I don't suggest you open it in my office or even at your desk, as you can see it's clearly marked. Wait until you get to your apt. And whatever instructions you have I don't want to know about them." "Abby, This looks like this one is entirely on you., So whatever your next assignment is good luck."

Abby returned to her apartment. She poured herself a cup of coffee, sat down on her couch and proceeded to open the envelop. Nervously anticipating what may be in it.

Inside the envelop was a set of orders and a letter from General Lancaster Thomas. She laid the orders aside and began to read the letter.

From the Desk of: *Brigadier General Lancaster Thomas (COUSAF-SRD)*

To: *Abigail Thorn (CIA– AIC)*

Abby it's been a few years since we last met and I hope that you remember me. We both worked on the Al-Hazreed case together and I assured you that it was in the best interest of all involved that we went ahead with the Kill order. Of course, at the time it was our only option and though the mission didn't pan out as we planned it did however end up being successfully accomplished. We managed to take out Al-Hazreed and it did put a strong and effective end to several future terrorist acts.

Your work in this case was invaluable to me and I can imagine by your new title you, like myself received a promotion and a position of higher responsibility. Here's where I need to call upon your services again.

With the successful JSOC/CIA operation, I was put in charge of the Research and Development Department at the Pentagon, and our department came into possession of some very important documentation which, held information on the development of some very controversial scientific inventions.

We were able to duplicate one of these inventions and also, we are now ready to put this invention which could change the world as we know it into action.

So, what I would like from you and the reason I asked for your transfer is for you to become my aide, and liaison for this project. This is an exciting and new position that was developed with your particular skill set in mind and can get you back in the field. .

I'm anxious to hear from you and look forward to seeing you in the next 4 days. I apologize for the short notice, but it is extremely crucial that I get you involve ASAP. There will be a ticket awaiting you at the train station in Chicago.

Brigadier General Lancaster Thomas (COUSAF-SRD)

So, two days later Abby Finds herself sitting at a table in the Chicago train station waiting for her train to head into D.C. Her mind racing a mile a minute. She is partly hoping that this new job with the General would result in her being able to find out the answers to her parents' deaths as well as give her the opportunity to work in the field again rather than sitting behind a desk.

Chapter 13

Saul and Abby board the train in Chicago. They both decide that they'd meet up in the observation deck for a couple of drinks and some more conversation. After a few hours passed in pleasant conversation a couple of drinks and a few games of cards they arrived in D.C. It was around 1730 so neither would make their appointment. So, they agreed to meet up for dinner and then they retired to their individual hotels.

After checking into their hotels, Saul, and Abby both thought about their trip. There was something familiar about the other to each of them but neither could pinpoint what exactly. Saul dismissed it as merely being in the right place at the right time.

Saul poured himself a scotch and re-read the letter from General Thomas one more time. "So, I'm actually going to be the first person ever to test the time machine out" "What a wonderful opportunity for me to experience everything I've ever dreamed of." "I always wondered what it would be like to live in the past. Now I'm going to have the opportunity to do so."

Meanwhile across town, Abby is trying to determine exactly what is going on. You see Abby never took anything at face value. All her life she questioned everything, and she wasn't going to stop now. "It's awful funny that the General would request me specifically, I know we have a past and all, but still and all why would he make me his aid?" "He's got to be trying to hide something." "I wonder if it has to do with the Al-Hazreed fiasco?"

"There is something really fishy going on here, I can feel it, but I can't put my finger on it exactly." "But at least this will give me the opportunity to get justice for my parents." "I know the bombing of the embassy in Cairo had something to do with Al-Hazreed, but it went higher than that." "And because of the kill order I was unable to get the intel I needed to find out more."

"I don't know exactly what the General knows but I sure the hell am going to find out." "As they say, keep your friends close and your enemies closer, and right now I don't consider the General a friend at all." "He knows something, and I will find out what it is." "The General was too eager to pursue the kill order on Hazreed. We could have easily done a snatch and grab, but of course I had to clear everything in that op with the White House, which meant involving JSOC." "Why did the General decide that the kill order would be the most viable?" "And I noticed none of the papers were recovered from the scene." "I didn't get the opportunity to return after I found out it was a hospital." "I seriously thought that it was an Al-Qaeda operation center. Had I have known it was a hospital I would have done things a hell of a lot different." "The general told me that day that if there was any collateral damage, he'd take care of it." " And why wasn't anything done after the fact like an investigation.?" "This whole situation stinks." "And I'll get to the bottom of it. "I've been looking for a reason to investigate this quietly without anyone knowing, and this may be my only chance to do so."

Abby takes a shower freshens up and then calls Saul, Saul answered his phone. "Hi Saul, this is Abby. Are we still on for dinner tonight? I know a great Italian restaurant here in D.C. where the food is out of this world." "Hey Abby, sure we're on for dinner and you're not talking about Giorgio's on U Street, are you?" "As a matter of fact, yes I am." "Yeah, I eat there every time I'm in town actually their veil marsala is to die for." "Well, I'm just about ready here how 'bout we meet there say around 8:30? I'll call ahead to get us a table," :Sounds good! See ya then."

Abby gets into her cab and heads out to meet with Saul. "What the fuck are you doing Abby?" "You gave your number to a perfect stranger, and it wasn't a burner number either." "Have you absolutely lost your mind?" "Well, he may not be perfect, but he is kind of cute."

Abby normally wasn't distracted by situations. She was used to thinking on the fly. What about this particular person has her dropping her guard.? "Well damned if I'm sure now but guaranteed I'm not letting my guard down again." "Stick to your cover story Abby the less he knows the better" "Plus he's just a professor and a civilian, There is no need to put him in any situations which may cause him injury.".

Saul met up with Abby at Giorgio's. They

both arrived promptly which to both their delight was a good thing. They were seated by the Maître De and ordered their drinks. Saul recommended a good chianti; Abby was stunned because she was going to suggest the exact same beverage. When the Waiter stepped up to take their order, they were both actively engaged in conversation, and neither were speaking English. They ordered their meals in perfect Italian. Saul ordered Velo Marsala [1]and Abby ordered, Parmigiana di vitello e Linguine con salsa di vongole veraci.[2]

[1] *Veal Marsala.* [2]*Veal Parmigiana and Linguini with white clam sauce.*

Chapter 14

After a delightful dinner, in each other's company they both bid each other farewell. Just as they were getting ready to depart, Abby excused herself and said she had to use the facilities. As she passed their waiter, she handed the waiter her credit card. When the waiter arrived at the table to clear it Saul asked him for the check. The waiter smiled and said, "The lady took care of it." "Have a great day."

Saul was astounded but pleasantly amused. "I guess she was just paying me back for lunch." Saul left the restaurant soon afterwards and headed back to his hotel. He wondered if he would ever get to see her again or if this was just a passing thing. Something however was bothering Saul as he headed back. She was somehow familiar to him, but he could not place from whence or where.

Saul arrived at the Pentagon the following morning. He was sitting in the reception room of the General's office drinking coffee waiting for the General to call him in. 30 minutes later Abby walks in. "What are you doing here?" "Are you tailing me?" Is this some kind of setup?" "I can't believe it, of all the things I've ever done, how could I have been so stupid?" "I knew there was no way in hell it was a chance meeting". "And to think I even agreed to have dinner with you."

"Hold on, wait a damn minute here." "First off what do you mean tailing you?" "You arrived here after I did." "Second, You told me you were an Executive Assistant for an advertising agency." "The Pentagon doesn't advertise shit." "So, what are you doing here.?" If anyone is being tailed, it's me."

The General's secretary is sitting behind her desk trying to keep a straight face. The argument between both Abby and Saul continued for at least a good 8 minutes. A com came across the secretary's desk, "I see they both have arrived." "Send them both in before there is a war in my lobby." The secretary then pipes up. The General will see you both now.

"Sit down the both of you!" "Apparently you two already know each other so introductions aren't necessary". "Well not really general we met in Chicago at the train station." "I really don't know her that well apparently even after lunch and dinner." "Did you send her to follow me to make sure I made it here?"

"Follow You? I seriously doubt that" "I don't think you're even a civilian and who you say you are." I was given orders to report here, and I guess Sir. You sent someone to make sure I did so."

"Both of you stop right there." "I sent for both of you individually because I have a job for both of you. I didn't know you were even going to meet each other until now." "Now both of you this is not a set up." "But since I have you both here, I might as well tell you both why I have summoned you."

"Saul Millings, meet Agent Abigail Thorn." "Now that formal introductions are out of the way." "Let's get down to the real reasons I sent for you both." "Saul you already know why you're here. You are going to be the very first person since H.G. Wells to travel through time." "WHAT!?", declared Abby abashedly. "Time Travel that's impossible". "Not anymore it isn't, and Saul is in a unique position to be able to work in that capacity. He is a history professor with a Doctorate, and I'm sure he won't interfere with the timeline." Abby was taken aback;

Saul was telling the truth the whole time. "And you Abigail will also be time travelling. Once Saul runs the initial test on the machine, I will be teaming you both up together." Your linguistic capabilities are invaluable as we're not entirely sure when and where we will be placing you both on the timeline. " Abby at this point said, "NO WAY IN HELL." I'm not going to do any of this". "I'm out of here." "SIT DOWN." You haven't a choice Abby you're under orders. I assume you read the orders right." "Well not fully, I assumed." "Well, this is a direct order, and you work for me now." "So, I don't want any more bullshit from either of you it's time to get you both up to speed."

"After we get you both into Medical for physicals and also to be fitted with a tracking device which we have developed in order for us to monitor you in whatever time and location you end up in. We will be sending you both on your first mission. And that is to find H.G. Wells and bring him back here." "Here's the catch, you cannot interfere with the current events on any timeline. You must find him and convince him to come back here with you." "Now Saul, I assume you have never met your great-grandfather therefore, we shouldn't have any interference in him recognizing you even by accident." "Great-Grandfather?" "You mean to tell me Saul is related to H.G. Wells." "As a matter of fact, he is." "Anyway find H.G. bring him back here safely so we can find out how much he actually knows about our timeline." "If you discover that the course of history is being interrupted in any way you both must figure out a way to correct it. But must do so without causing any troubles within history."

"This is where it might be difficult and tricky. Other than your trackers, you mustn't carry with you any devices which may indicate you're from a different time." "You must both be able to adapt to the time your in." "This is where your skill set comes into play Abby." "You have to train Saul to maintain a cover story yet follow Saul's lead as to the course of the events in history." "Any interference can result in temporal paradoxes which can interfere with the current timeline and thus changing the events here as well."

"We are assuming that since H.G. is already a time traveler that bringing him to the current time will not alter history in any way." "We're hoping that by sending you two out there we can maintain that same condition. After we ran several tests, we noted that, as long as nothing was removed from the time periods time seemed to stay relatively normal. We need to keep it that way."

"As we send you back into individual periods you will be provided with accurate clothing and accoutrements that suit the timelines, we send you to. This is to ensure that you fit in and that we don't have to have you both discovered as time travelers. In addition, we will be giving you for each trip a limited number of hours to search. You must return to the machine on time. Any mistakes can be disastrous. Are we clear about your mission?"

Saul was ecstatic. He definitely wanted to do this. This was his opportunity to experience all those era's he taught about. He could imagine when this was all over how much better his lectures would be because he'd be able to give firsthand information about the periods he talks about. Abby was slightly more reluctant. She could see the importance of the mission, and well it would be an adventure. Plus, it might give her a chance to research her parents' death and find out what she really wanted to know. So, they both agreed to the mission.

Saul and Abby reported to Medical. They both went through a complete physical, and afterwards both had a microchip implanted into their right shoulder. After the microchip was thoroughly tested to make sure that the readings from it were accurate, they reported back to General Thomas.

The microchips read heart rate, respirations, pulse oxygenation, and blood pressure. In addition, it also read the exact date time and location. This chip then sent all its information to Central Command. It was designed to ensure that not only would Central Command be able to keep track of them but also maintain and monitor their health conditions and send needed materials if necessary to them.

This chip was also attached to a small holographic ring which each of them wore on their finger. When out in the field they too could monitor their location and the location of the drops and the time machine as well as the time so that they could return to the machine on schedule. If either of them failed to return the machine would return to the current time without them and have to be resent. This could actually take a little over 24 hours for them to recalibrate the machine. So, returning to the machine on time was of vital importance.

The tracking device also had one other feature. It could trace anomalies in the timeline. Thus, allowing Saul and Abby to either extract themselves if they were the cause, or they could work to correct the anomaly and complete their mission. Their first and foremost mission of course was strictly observational other than to recover H.G. And with no sure way of knowing where or when H.G. was this mission would be a difficult one. Because they'd have to trace each timeline within approximate decades.

Abby and Saul sat in the cafeteria and tried to decide where and when to go first. The General told them to have their decision by the end of day. Now with their mission in mind their thoughts of the previous morning had passed. No longer arguing with each other they knew they had to work together. So, they decided that the first thing they needed to do was find common ground.

       With formal introductions out of the way. Saul and Abby decided that they needed to find common ground.   If they were going to work together, they better at least get to know each other on a more personal level than just two acquaintances that met on a train. Abby suggested that they start with their childhood histories. If they were going to be able to create back stories for themselves, they needed some basis in fact to work off of so that they could keep their alter egos fresh in their minds when they begin their mission. Saul agreed being he had no experience being anything but himself.

Chapter 15

So, Saul, while being interviewed by Abby began to tell his life story . "Where and when were you born?" "I was born on June 27, 1986, at Herrick Memorial Hospital in Berkeley California." "My mother died at childbirth, and I was raised by my father, so I never really got to know my mother." "What did your father do for a living?" "My father was a curator at The Phoebe A Hearst Museum of Anthropology" "So I kind of grew up with a love of history and studying the origin of mankind." "Is this what led to your current occupation at Stanford?" "Yeah, I guess you can say that." "Being I was always fascinated with history, I started studying it all throughout grade school all the way into college where I decided to pursue my degrees in History and Anthropology."

"So, I'm assuming you also studied foreign languages as well?" "My foreign languages studies began in high school and stemmed throughout college, but I always seemed to have a knack for picking up languages. So, while researching ancient texts I started work on translations" "You were able to speak Farsi and understand it quite well when we were at the train station." "What other languages do you speak?" "With a little bit of fluency, I speak, German, English, Spanish, French, Italian, Gaelic, Russian, Hebrew, and Arabic." "I can read and translate most other foreign languages including those of the Cyrillic, and Ideograms." "Well, that could definitely come in handy for us when we travel through time." "Do you have any other interests we should know about?" "Well, I do like archeology, and I collect artifacts." "Well that we will have to be careful about, you remember what the General said about making sure nothing gets removed from any of the timelines." "So, when did you find out you were related to H.G. Wells?" "I actually discovered that by accident." "I was researching my own genealogy when I made the discovery that on my mother's side apparently my Great Grandmother was one of his many lovers." "And having read the book the Time Machine and always wondering about it I began collecting all of his works". "Just to be clear, you have never met your great grandfather correct. Yeah, he died in 1946 so I never had the opportunity to know him." "Is your father still alive?" "Sorry I had to ask that question." "No, it's okay he passed away when I turned 22, so basically I've been on my own since college." "How did he die if I may ask?" "He died of natural causes he had a heart attack." "Have you ever done any role-playing or played any RPGs like Dungeon and Dragons?" "Back in high school yes. I rather enjoyed that aspect of trying to live in fictional and historical worlds." "Well Saul all this information can easily lead a backstory and cover story for you. Because you really have no reason to change up any of it except when we travel through time, we will probably have to make sure we're assumed from that time period." "This is where you're going to be a huge asset and have an advantage over me." "You may have to teach me a brief history on the fly" "Could you do that?" "Of course. I shouldn't have a problem."

Then it was Saul's turn to question Abby. "So, Abby first question for you, where were you born?" "I really don't know; I was adopted as an infant." "When were you born?" "June 28, 1986" "So we are the same age?" "Apparently" "Are you're adopted parents still alive?" Actually, no they were killed in Cairo in 2008." "So, when you were growing up where did you live?" "Well, because my parents were analyst for the Department of the Interior we moved from embassy to embassy throughout my childhood.". "So, I assume you picked up foreign languages from travelling place to place.?" "Yes." "What languages do you speak?" "French, Farsi obviously, German, Greek, Italian, Latin, Chinese, Japanese, Russian, and Spanish." "If we had to pick up another language while travelling, could you adapt and learn that language quickly?" "Yes, I have a knack for linguistics" "What was your current occupation prior to coming to work with me?" "I really cannot answer that question. I worked for the government. Was hired right out of high school." "Well now that we know each other a little better I think we better report back to the General and let's plan our first mission together." "I'm sorry about earlier honestly I wasn't following you or tailing you." "And now I know that our meeting was strictly a bit of kismet." "That's okay, I understand and I'm sorry about accusing you it's just my occupation and work for the Government makes me a bit paranoid."

Saul and Abby reported back to the

General. General Thomas escorted them down to the laboratory and Saul boarded the machine. He was ready to make his first solo. The lab techs did all the final checks and over the com Saul heard the general command him to set the machine for 20 minutes ahead of the current time with the lab as the destination. A countdown commenced and Saul engaged the machine. There was a slight pop and a bang and Saul jumped forward in time. When he arrived, things were pretty much the same as when he left except the technicians were analyzing all the data sent via the tracker. Meanwhile back in the current time the machine vanished, and they were waiting for his reappearance. After twenty minutes there was another slight pop and bang the machine was back and Saul walked into the lab door. "WOW! Talk about déjà vu. Except I already experienced this after I left." "Are you feeling okay Saul?" Yeah, I'm fine a little disorientated but nothing I can't really adjust to. Other than that, I'm perfectly fine.

Chapter 16

Saul had successfully made the jump. He felt confident afterwards that indeed it was not only feasible to jump through time, but that it had no ill effects on the body except minor disorientation. So, it was now Abby's turn the same experiment was run and Abby experienced the exact same things. Moving forward in time was easy because the events hadn't actually occurred until after the fact. But going backwards would be trickier because again they ran the risk of running into themselves. Therefore, rather than experiment with it. They decided it would be better just to go ahead and do it and take their chances.

So, they all went back to the office to discuss when and where they would be headed first. Where and when would be the best time to find H.G. and bring him back to the future with them. Saul suggested they start where it all began. He had done research on the Renaissance and realized that Leonardo Da Vinci had experimented with time travel himself. Although not successfully because he didn't have the materials to build the machine. Saul wondered if somehow his grandfather had managed to get ahold of the initial plans of Leonardo's and had completed the experiments. Around about the time he wrote *The Time Machine.*

So, what if they go back to the Renaissance and try to figure out how H.G. got his hands on Leonardo's works. Saul explained the history of Leonardo's work to the General and they all agreed that this would be the best course of action.

Meanwhile, in 1865 H.G. Wells is working on the plans for the new time machine. The prototype obviously had failed he must have forgotten the fail safes and when he was calibrating the chronograph it had made a jump. He wasn't aware however that the machine had not even jumped but had literally vanished. The continuum was interrupted by H.G. when he landed in the same time period.

H.G. had to find the time machine or the prototype. He remembered that he had built two machines, one of which failed and the other which of course succeeded. If he could find the machine, he could go back in time again and convince himself not to build it.

But he couldn't remember when he built the second machine. One of the hazards of multiple trips through the space/time continuum is a loss of memory due to disorientation. Short term memory wasn't as affected as long term was. So, remembering when something happened exactly would prove to be difficult.

So, the first place he decided to go would be to his laboratory where he had hidden away Leonardo's papers. If he could change the location of the papers and hide them elsewhere his other self wouldn't have possession of them thus be unable to complete the project.

But when was his other self, going to be there? So, for 16 days H.G. very discreetly wandered around town staying at various hostels under assumed identities, carefully surveilling his other self so he could get a feel for his routine. When H.G. Wells wasn't going to be at his lab he'd steal the papers and take off in the prototype. He'd make all the necessary adjustments to travel into the future so that the prototype would be available to him.

Once he chose a future location, he would then complete the machine, hide in another time, and never leave it again. If he stole the prototype and the papers the other Him could not build the machine. His other self without the papers would abandon the machine and the project entirely and would just write a book about it. Called *The Chronic Argonauts*.

Saul and Abby prepared themselves for their trip to the Renaissance after donning period clothing, familiarizing themselves with period Italian, and determining when and where they would land the machine so that they could not easily be discovered was all planned out. They worked for days just on making sure everything would be properly prepared. There would be no room for mistakes. One mistake could potentially alter history. And as for the taking of the plans from Leonardo that too would alter history . So, they had to make sure that Leonardo's plans stay in one place. The holo–rings were also equipped with a camera. They could take pictures inconspicuously of the plans and be able to bring the photos back with them so the time machine could be built in their own future, without disrupting the timeline.

Chapter 17

A set of rules was discussed with the General regarding time travel and the best methods of maintaining the timelines as well as allowing for the amount of time anyone could stay in a particular time period without disrupting the continuum. Saul sat down for several nights compiling the following rules and presented them to the General for final approval.

Rules for Time Travel

1. A traveler must never interfere with the timeline. He/she must adapt to the current timeline and act accordingly .

2. A traveler must be equipped with the proper period clothing and accoutrements. They must appear to be citizens of the timeline they are in and must be able to pass as same.

3. A traveler must be versed in many languages and dialects. and be able to speak to them as if they are natives.

4. When assuming an identity a traveler must always prepare themselves with appropriate common

names and commit these names to memory.

5. The traveler must study the history of the time period he/she is entering. They must familiarize themselves with the location, the availability of housing etc.

6. A traveler must not reside in the same timeline for a period over 90 days. They must return to their individual timelines at no later than the close of a year after they arrived.

7. The machine will be set upon landing to return to command and will be re-sent by command 24 hours to the appropriate time period after the period of the 90 days is up. Failure of a traveler to return to the time machine can result in hazardous complications for both the traveler and the command so being prompt in arriving back at the machine is vital. The Command will send back the machine 2 weeks afterwards if the deadline is missed. You must return to it.

8. Nothing is ever to be taken from any timeline in physical form. You may only take with you what you arrived with.

9. Travelers may have to interact in the timeline in order to fit in but remember your primary mission is being an observer. You cannot interfere with events that could alter the future. Be cautious as to how much you associate with others, do not establish personal relationships, etc.

10. If you detect an anomaly in the timeline you must endeavor to correct it. However, you must make this correction carefully and can only alter events in that instance to adjust to the recorded history of the events.

11. Remember above all else what you do in the past can and will affect the future.

Once Saul established these guidelines, he then presented them to the General. The general then approved of them and made Saul and Abby heads of the time corp. Though many times they would be forced to stay in the current time monitoring and training troops they would be sent on missions as well.

The most important missions of course were the ones that they would take priority of. And their first mission was to be of vital importance. They were to be sent to recover copies of the documents of Leonardo Da Vinci. This was to ensure that the time machine would be built and also to insure the future of the time corp. Of course, on a side note they were also to try to find H.G. Wells and bring the traveler back to the current time, or they were to assassinate him on the exact date he was alleged to have died   so that he himself could not interfere with the timeline either.

The General of course had an ulterior motive. He didn't want to be exposed regarding the Hazreed incident, and in addition he was hiding other secrets. Secrets that could cost him his career and his very life if they were ever to come out. Once the General had realized the implications of time travelling, he also construed that the alterations of time itself could change the course of modern history, and his very existence and current situation depended on maintaining the course they were on.

Seemingly the only people he could trust were Saul and Abby and the Lieutenant Colonel who worked on the Al Hazreed case with him. He had to maintain the highest level of security and secrecy about this project and made sure that he personally did not divulge any information that could jeopardize him in any way.

Chapter 18

H.G. Landed his machine in the Ardennes and traveled south till he reached Grenoble he was travelling carefully, and he spotted a French nobleman which was around his same height. While the nobleman had stopped his carriage to take a respite from the weeks travel, he stole quietly to the carriage and rode off with it. When he got a few miles down the road he stopped the carriage donned the nobleman's clothing and made his way to Nice.

Upon arriving in Nice he read the letters the nobleman was carrying and assumed his identity. He became the Count of Saintonge. While travelling through Nice he of course availed himself of all the privileges afforded a noble, housing, food, and even the privileges afforded by the courtesans of the time.

There he met a courtesan who he favored by the name of Lissette Auberee. After spending numerous hours in her company, enjoying the pleasures that she afforded him he invited her to come along with him to Italy. Lissette was happy to oblige. Soon the companions traveled to Milan where in order to avoid any semblance of impropriety H.G. would declare her his niece.

H.G. had arranged by letter while he was in France to commission Leonardo to do a painting of his Niece for him. His real reason of course was to be able to get an individual audience with Leonardo so that while he was distracted, he could abscond with the plans for the time machine. This was the year 1503.

He got a response back from Leonardo saying he'd be happy to do a portrait of his niece for him for the price of 15 Lira. So, he and Lissette headed to Milan. During the journey of course they enjoyed each other's company, and they paid their driver enough money to keep his mouth shut.

They arrived in Milan and H.G. rented a room in the Hostel. It would be at least a week before his appointment with Leonardo and he would in the meantime continue to maintain his cover.

Saul and Abby arrived in a vineyard around Florence Their machine disappeared the moment they stepped off of it. Everything was going according to schedule. They would have 90 days to complete the mission. They were both hoping that they would find H.G. Wells within Milan and try to stop him from taking the manuscripts.

Saul's study of Leonardo was enough for him to know the exact address in Milan where Leonardo had his studio. There was a Hostel a few streets over where they could both stay and there was an inn where Leonardo would spend many of his nights eating dinner. When he wasn't at Sforza Palace.

While in his apartment at the hostel Saul began to paint, he focused his paintings on birds in flight and landscapes. He knew that Leonardo was obsessed with flying and figured it would be a quick way to engage him in conversation. The other paintings he attempted were portraits. In four days, Saul completed 8 paintings they were not too bad but definitely inadequate by the standards of the day.

Abby in the meantime got herself a job working as a scullery maid in the inn where Leonardo dined. She figured it would be an ideal way to meet up with Leonardo and engage him in conversation while serving him. Once she established a rapport with him, she would then convince him to attend to Saul.

Saul and Abby took the names Alessandro and Alessandra Baldovinetti as their assumed identities. Brother and sister from Florence, Who were both in Milan to pursue Alessandro's love of painting. They both hoped that Alessandro would be able to learn from Maestro Da Vinci. And that he'd become a known artist.

This was their cover story and so far, things were working as planned. Several nights in a row Alessandra served Da Vinci and struck up conversation with him. She told him of her brother and asked if he would like to see some of his paintings. Maestro Da Vinci said that he would find the time to come view the paintings and he scheduled the viewing two days later.

Chapter 19

Abby went back to the hostel and met up with Saul. She informed Saul that in two days' time he will have a visit with Leonardo Da Vinci. Saul was fully prepared for the visit. He made sure to strategically place his paintings where they would best catch Leonardo's eye.

"Not bad at all Saul, I didn't know you were a painter." "Well, I took a couple of art classes in my spare time figured in my line of work it'd come in handy." "Well, it definitely came in handy for this mission. Your skills are good enough to catch the attention of the Maestro." "I sincerely hope so, and I hope they pique his interest enough to get him to show me his drawings."

"I'm sure they will." "Well, he should be arriving around half past two. I am supposed to meet him at the inn and escort him here." "Well. We shall see you then." "You still remember your cover, right?" "Yep, I'm your brother Alessandro and I came to Milan to study painting under the masters."

Two days later.

Abby went back to the inn and around a quarter to two Maestro Da Vinci arrived for lunch. He was served by Abby, and they proceeded to chat a little while before both left and headed for the Hostel. When they arrived at the apartment Saul was already busy working on another painting. He was painting terns on the rocks of the shoreline.

"Maestro, I would like to introduce you to my brother Alessandro." "It's a pleasure to meet you Alessandro." "Your sister has been telling me a great deal about your paintings and I see you are working on one now."

"Indeed, well she speaks as if I'm a master but I'm nowhere near enough qualified to be considered in that capacity." Leonardo scanned the room. "Let me be the judge of that." "By your leave Maestro, and please do tell me the truth." "For I wish to become better and from what I've been told there is none better in all of Italy than that of your honorable self." "Now you flatter me." "No, I only speak truthfully."

"Alessandro let us then start with the one you are working on right now." "You are a naturalist in your style as I can perceive, however you are making the one mistake that many have made." "You are painting from memory and not from nature herself." "Your shadows aren't falling in the proper places. This occurs when you can't visually see the objects you are painting, and you are painting by your memory of same." "This is causing your paintings to appear two dimensional. Yes, there is beauty in them however, they have no depth. Shadow and the knowledge of the reflection and refraction of light over distance is of vital importance because it allows one to perceive all the dimensions uniformly, height, breadth, and width. Within your paintings I see height and width but no breadth." "If I may show you here what I mean?" "By all means Maestro it would be my honor." Leonardo took an apple from out of the fruit bowl; he placed it in front of the fruit bowl and placed the candle approximately eighteen degrees and eight inches from it. He then proceeded to take a charcoal and drew the apple and provided the shadow surrounding it. Saul immediately noticed the difference from Leonardo's apple and his own. "Thank you Maestro I can see exactly what you mean now." Leonardo just smiled.

"Alessandro, I have also noticed your portraits. If I may mention to you, they are disproportionate please forgive me." "I have a portrait to do of a French nobleman's niece commissioned in four days' time. Would you like to sit in on this portrait as my apprentice?" "Maestro it would be my privilege to do so as I know I need ample instruction on portraits for they are not my strongest suit." "Come to my studio in four days and we shall work on this portrait together."

Saul remembered that the most famous portrait Leonardo ever painted was the Mona Lisa. He could barely contain himself. "Was he, actually going to meet the model for the Mona Lisa and know of its origin?" "His mind began racing about a mile a minute." Saul, of course agreed to attend this painting with exuberance. Almost too much exuberance but he caught himself.

Leonardo bowed and took his leave.

Chapter 20

Two days later H.G. and Lissette arrived in Milan. They both rented rooms suitable for nobles and proceeded to enjoy the accommodations. That very evening around five o'clock H.G walked to Leonardo's academy. The Classes were just letting out so basically all that were left present were Leonardo and a few students. Including Saul, who was at the time just finishing up some final touches on the still life he was working on.

When H.G. walked into the studio, Saul recognized him almost immediately. It was hard not to take notice. The man's mannerisms just weren't exactly suitable for the time period. And the resemblance to the photos which Saul had of his great grandfather was uncanny.

Saul turned his ring and turned on the camera for recording. He figured he might as well get some surveillance footage on H.G. to see what he was actually up to. He knew that H.G. would be after the manuscript but was not sure how he was going to go about getting it.

H.G approached Leonardo. "Good day sir I

am Count De Saintonge I received your reply dispatch, And we left a bit early in case of weather, road conditions or scoundrels on the road we did not want to be late. This portrait will mean a lot to my family so we are a couple of days early and we can begin any time you are ready." "Well, It's a pleasure to meet you Count" "It is more my honor to meet you sir." So, you wish me to paint a portrait of your niece I understand." "Yes, Sir that is correct". "You are aware I do charge a fee I have expenses." "Of course, sir you quoted me 15 lira I have 8 with me to set as a deposit so you know I am serious. "Well, I would like to meet this young lady, if I may, is she with you may I ask?" "No Sir after the long trip she is at the hostel getting refreshed and rested for tomorrow, as I promised to show her your beautiful city." "Then perhaps we can meet for breakfast at 7 o'clock." "Beg to please, can we allow the young lady to sleep in and perhaps meet at 9 instead.?" "Yes, that is suitable to me." "Perhaps then we can start on the portrait the following day."

"Certainly, we can definitely do that." "Excellent you have such a lovely town and I do want her to see it before we head back."

"And Sir you Hail from Nice.? She is from Nice; I am from Grenoble. " "Grenoble is such a lovely place I've been there." "Each town has its own beauty and beauties." "I could not agree more sir." "Would you mind if my protégé, Alessandro attended breakfast with us.?" "Absolutely not may I inquire as to why however?" "I wish to teach him the interview process." "Ahh Excellent, I'm sure it will be a very valuable lesson for him."

"Alessandro please join us for a moment." "Yes Maestro, how may I Be of service to you.?" I'd like you to meet the Count de Saintonge. "The count has commissioned me to paint his niece's portrait." "Excellent the Maestro has been giving me instruction on portrait painting and now I get to see the Maestro at work." "Would you be willing to join us for breakfast tomorrow, I wish to teach you the interview process." "Indeed, it would be an honor to share a breakfast with you."

"Then I shall see you all tomorrow and bid you adieu." I look forward to the meeting Maestro."

Saul returned to the hostel and met up with Abby. "You're not going to believe the intel I just got. I do believe I've found our mark and sure enough he's definitely in this time period and most likely after the plans." "Have you yourself managed to get eyes on the plans." "No unfortunately I have not. It's common knowledge in our time period that Leonardo used invisible ink on some of his drawings and his manuscripts. I'm afraid this might be one of those occasions ." So, our best course of action would be tail H.G. and see if indeed he snatches the drawings and then take him then. "

"Actually, Saul that's not a good Idea. I really got to thinking after you left. I re-read the rules which you set forth regarding time travel and which of course made sense." "We really cannot interfere with the timeline". "We're going to have to let him steal the plans." And if we are going to capture him it will have to be in his own timeline." "So let me see what intel you have gathered."

Saul turned on the holo projection and he and Abby viewed and listened to the conversation. "Indeed, it appears that He is in the vicinity." "You're supposed to meet him and his niece for breakfast." I would suggest that you have breakfast at the inn where I work. This way we can both be present to gain intel." :We know Leonardo frequents it, so should not be an issue for him to arrange the meeting there." "In fact, it wouldn't surprise me at all because it's his favorite eating place."

Chapter 21

The following morning Saul arrives at the academy around eight in the morning. He figured not only could he get an early start, but he could also find the ideal location to place his holo ring to record the events of the day. The night before Abby informed him that the rings could hold ten terabytes of data so there wouldn't be an issue him recording the events at the studio.

Saul readied himself, place the ring and his cuffs on the workbench where, by chance the manuscripts were also placed. It was the most secure place in the studio to avoid getting any unwanted paint or charcoal on clothing or items of importance. Saul then decided to get to work on a recent drawing.

Leonardo entered the studio. "Good morrow Alessandro, I see you have arrived early." "Indeed, Maestro I wanted to get a start on this drawing of the Palazzo di Sforza" I made some notes where the shadows would be placed so I could maximize the perspective." "Well done, Alessandro." You Have been paying attention to my instructions."

"And you have chosen a fine subject for your next work." "After breakfast we can focus more on this work, and I'll show you some of my other buildings." "There is a different technique you will learn when doing buildings as opposed to naturals."

'Come my dear Alessandro we mustn't tarry too long, for we must also meet with the Count and Contessa soon." "Indeed Maestro, we must. " "And I am looking much forward to this meeting because I would like to know how to interview for portraits."

As they were walking to the inn, Leonardo explained to Alessandro the importance of interview the models. "You see my young protégé the interview is important because it allows for us to understand the personality of the individual of which, we are painting." "You want to capture their personality, otherwise you are merely just painting a mask of them." "So, what the interview does is allows us to understand the individual and note some of the more non-descript quirks the person may have." "Like a twitch in the eye, or even a slight curve to the lips when they are disturbed by something."

Saul and Leonardo arrived at the inn at about eight forty-five. They sat at the table and ordered a quick repast of soup and ale and awaited their company's arrival. H.G. Arrived with a very attractive twenty-five year old woman which Saul immediately recognized as the Mona Lisa. Saul was ecstatic. He tried not to show his enthusiasm however but rather stayed seated across from her listening to his Maestro interview her.

Abby served their drinks and repast and also recognized Lissette as the Mona Lisa. She could see the look of excitement in Saul's face and when placing his order in front of him gave him a quick "HARUMPF". Saul took the hint from her and excused himself to utilize the restroom. Which of course was an outhouse out back. As soon as he got outside, he was approached by Abby. He quickly embraced her and spun her around. Abby pushed him off of her and said to him; "Now that you've got that out of your system, compose yourself I realize that's the Mona Lisa, and I   understand your excitement, but we have a job to do. And if you ever do that again You will be picking up your teeth, understand.?"   Saul apologized and regained his composure. They both went back inside at different times.

The repast was finished, and the parties agreed to meet the following day at the studio for the preliminary sketches. In the meantime, H.G was going to take Lissette on a tour of Milan. Saul ever so carefully followed H.G, and Lissette tailing them where they went. When he was spotted, he quickly used the excuse that he was searching himself for a building to paint for the Maestro.

H.G. accepted his explanations and asked if he'd like to join them on the rest of the trip around town. Saul of course said It would be his privilege and indeed joined them. Engaging them on the history of Milan and some of the sights they were to see.

Chapter 22

The next afternoon H.G. and Lissette arrive at the studio. Saul and Leonardo set up to do the preliminary sketches and to make sure they capture the right lighting and locations for the model to be at her best appearance. Leonardo explains to Saul that "in order to effectively paint a portrait the model has to maintain her position." So, every thirty minutes a break is allowed for, and the model can get up stretch or whatever he/she needs to do in order to not be cramped. Once the model returns from the break careful consideration must be given in order to for, he/she to return to the original pose and the lighting has to be readjusted so that the shadows fall precisely as before.

Saul was just happy to be sketching the Mona Lisa. Luckily, he had set up his camera yesterday because Had he not he may not have gotten the footage that they needed. Things were progressing at a normal pace, and nothing seemed to be happening but the painting. "Could I be wrong about H.G.'s plans?" Thought Saul to himself.

H.G. the whole time was surveilling the

room. He was looking at all the paintings, walking around to all the tables etc., His reasoning was simply act bored and nonchalant but at the same time locate the manuscript and figure out the best way to abscond with it. When the right opportunity presented itself, he would act and discretely get the page from the notebook.

H .G. knew exactly which page had the plans on it. He also knew that it was written in invisible ink, and that the only way for him to recover the plans was to remove the page. When he found the page, he would carefully take it from the manuscript. So, he had to have an absolute perfect time to do so.

Several hours passed with multiple breaks taken between. Lissette was starting to get bored and antsy. H.G. asked that his niece be able to take a break for lunch and they return after a repast. Leonardo seeing his model was beginning to squirm a bit and having gently chastised her twice, decided this would be a good idea.

He tells Saul to take her to lunch if she wouldn't mind his company. Saul was overjoyed. He had entirely forgot his mission at that point, and it was a good thing his camera was in place. "I trust that you will be a perfect gentleman young Alessandro." "But of course, sire." "Then I give you leave to take her for a repast."

This was the opportunity H.G. was looking for. He knew if he could get her out of the way and find a way to distract Master Leonardo, he could steal the plans and get out of there. H.G. didn't have to try hard to distract Leonardo. Leonardo was called up to the loft by another of his students. Apparently that student was having trouble mixing one of the mediums and needed his master's help.

Leonardo made his own paints and often created his own mixtures thus giving unique coloration to many of his works. So, when a student would have a problem getting the proportions correct, he would have to attend to it immediately.

This was H.G's opening. Leonardo headed upstairs and H.G. Stole over to the manuscript and carefully ripped out the page with the drawing on the back. He folded it carefully into a small bundle and when he was just about to pocket the bundle

Leonardo headed down the stairs. Quickly thinking he walked over to the Mona Lisa, palming the bundle picked it off the easily and stuffed the bundle between the wood frame and the canvas.

"Your Honorable Sir what are you doing with that it isn't finished." "I'm sorry I was just taking a closer look at it." "Truly you are capturing my niece's radiance quite well." "I'm indeed quite pleased." "In fact, I'm so pleased with this that I will pay you more than 15 lira for it." He placed the sketching back on the easel and offered Leonardo an additional 12 Lira. Leonardo declined and said, "No the 15 Lira we agreed upon has bound me as a gentleman and that is the price."

"Fair enough." At that moment Saul and Lissette walk back in. And after the repast, Leonardo and Saul got right back to work. The day passed and the preliminary sketches were completed. Saul's sketch was adequate, and his master was pleased with his work.

H.G. and Lissette left the studio. They headed back to the hostel quickly packed and sent for a dispatch, when the dispatcher arrived H.G.

informed him to inform Master Leonardo that they had been called away on a family emergency. And that they will return within 2 weeks to complete the sitting for the portrait. H.G. dropped Lissette in Nice and headed back to Grenoble and the time machine. He would recover the manuscript in the future because only he knows it's missing and where it is.

Chapter 23

Saul gathered his cuffs and ring and headed back to the hostel. H.G. had gotten away and he thought for sure that he had botched the mission. Saul was unable to secure the plans, he didn't know if H.G. actually had managed to get them as he wasn't there, all because he was enamored by the beauty of Lissette. So, with an air of despondency and defeat he returned. Abby arrived at the Hostel about 20 minutes later after her shift was up.

Saul broke the news to Abby. Abby at first was pissed but she said to Saul," I know you placed the camera let's look at the footage. "Saul took off his ring and turned on the video. The first couple of hours was footage of H.G. wandering around the studio. After studying H.G's movements for a few she realized what had happened. She watched H.G. take the manuscript when Leonardo went up the stairs and fold it neatly. Then she watched him holding the painting. She realized he must have placed the manuscript somewhere within the painting because he didn't have time to pocket it.

While watching the video a knock occurred

on the door of the room. They quickly turned off the video and answered the door. It was Leonardo and he was livid. "He explained to Saul that the painting probably wouldn't be completed because apparently the Count had a family emergency and sent dispatch to inform him, he would not be sure when he'd return.

At this point Saul and Abby realized they too would have to get out of there. So, After Leonardo left, they set their tracker for 48 hours,

The clock on their tracker was ticking down, they had only 11 hours left to return to the machine. Unable to completely watch the holo, They were ready to call the mission a botch. Then it occurred to Abby. It wasn't a failed mission at all. No, they didn't recover the plans and they were unable to do so. No, they didn't capture H.G., but the plans didn't fall into H.G.'s hands either they succeeded in preventing him from getting them in the current timeline. They checked the tracker for any anomalies. And according to the record there wasn't any anomalies present. Which means they didn't interfere with the timeline, the Mona Lisa would be painted eight years later and gifted to Francis I, and

Saul's drawings would be lost to obscurity. So, in a way the mission was actually a success.

Saul thought about it more too, he realized exactly when they could catch H.G., and it would be in the timeline which Would cause no risk for an anomaly to occur. Abby asked Saul, what he meant when he explained, "I know where and when we can recover the Manuscript and also H.G. and we won't risk disrupting the space time continuum."

"Do tell!" "Well obviously the Mona Lisa does get painted. Apparently, the plans are behind the Mona Lisa. And the next time the Mona Lisa gets stolen is the 29th of August 1939, it was right after France capitulated and the Nazi's took all the art to the Altaussee mine where it was later discovered and returned to the Louvre in 1945. So, our timeline indicates that he's going to be anywhere between 1939 to 1945. And we can work from there to figure out when and how we can get that manuscript and capture him."

"Well, we have to get back to command. We will inform the General of our findings when we get back and we'll figure out our next course of action from there." "That sounds good to me." "So, though the mission was a failed one it didn't exactly fail as nothing was taken from the timeline, no anomalies occurred, and we didn't lose the Mona Lisa". "That would be the conclusion I have to draw from this mission."   "I just hope that the General draws the same conclusion."

Saul and Abby return to the site of the machine 10 minutes before its scheduled arrival. They remained hidden until the machine arrived and boarded the machine. They set the chronograph to 2028 and the location to the command center, engaged the machine and reappeared at the center.

The General met them and noted that they didn't have H.G. with them nor did they have the plans. "What the Hell Happened?" I gave you 90 days and you're back in less than a month." "Do you think this is some form of a vacation or something?" "You had a job to do, and you failed to do your job."

Chapter 30

The General stormed off disgusted. He had not even bothered to let Saul and Abby explain. Saul and Abby returned to their hotel rooms. They were both disoriented and exhausted from the mission and just wanted to get back to their own semblance of normalcy for the time being. They would report again to the General in the next few days. And hopefully he will be in a better mood and willing to listen,

Saul and Abby were just about to leave when they were stopped by Lieutenant Colonel Spalding. "Wait a minute the both of you." "Obviously the General isn't in a mood to discuss the mission. However, unfortunately we need your after action report by no later than Thursday if you could get it to my email tonight, I'll forward it over to the General and perhaps by tomorrow he'll be a little more levelheaded." "Then I want you both to report in no later than Friday morning for debriefing." "Well Colonel, tell ya what, We'll get the report to you but don't expect to see either one of us until Friday afternoon, because I'm going to take and get out of these period clothes, hit a hot shower which I haven't had in over 3 weeks and go to sleep in an actual bed." "So, orders be damned I'll be here when I get here." Saul couldn't agree more.

Abby and Saul walked out of the office into the foyer, still wearing their period outfits. Fortunately, no one in the Pentagon paid them any heed, apparently people working in the pentagon are used to seeing strange things. "They hopped into individual cabs and headed back to their hotels. When they got into the cabs the cab drivers asked about the weird clothing and they both just replied, "Renaissance Festival".

As soon as they got back to their hotels both immediately hopped into the shower and then got into their regular clothes. Afterwards since it was mid-afternoon, they both laid down in their beds and took a nap. Saul's phone rang it was Abby on the other end. "Hey Saul", "Hi Abby". "I realize I probably woke you up just got up myself as a matter of fact. But we have to get that after action report done. Do you want to meet at my hotel room we'll order Chinese and watch the holo vid again and piece together our report.?"

"Sounds good to me I can meet up with you a five o'clock if that will work for you?" "Yeah, that'll be fine". "I'm in room 517. and I'm staying at the Washington Plaza Hotel." "Okay Abby, I'll see you then." "And by the way working with you was actually quite enjoyable." "Thanks, I can say the same to you. We do make a pretty good team, don't we?" "Indeed, we do!"

Saul took a cab to the hotel where Abby was staying. He arrived in the hotel lobby, went to the elevator, and proceeded to the 5th floor. He knocked on Abby's door. Abby let him inside and they sat down at the table. Saul and Abby played back the entire holo and spent the evening typing up the after action report while eating their food. They then sent the report to the Lt. Colonel's email and spent the rest of the evening until the wee hours of the morning chatting.

Saul informed Abby about his plan to capture H.G. There would be no better way to do it than to go back to 1939 and try to intercept the plans from the Mona Lisa before the fall of Paris.

And of course, they would lay a trap for H.G. in order to capture him. With this plan in mind, they wouldn't be caught off guard again.

Abby reminded Saul however, that H.G. Had to gain possession of the plans in order to build the time machine and place the copy of the plans in his own notebook. It would be better if they let him get the plans maintain surveillance on him and let the first time machine be built. This would maintain the integrity of the timeline. Afterwards they could capture him and secure the plans themselves. Thus, avoiding temporal disruption.

After spending hours in discussion on what they needed to do they finally came up with a plan to present to the General. They just hoped that the General would be calmed down and willing to listen to reason. Saul bid Abby farewell, and then took a cab back to his hotel and went promptly to sleep.

It would be around noon when Abby woke up and called Saul and said "Shit, we need to report to command." Saul, responded groggily, "Yeah Yeah I'm up I'll get dressed and head out see you in about 40 minutes."

Chapter 31

After a lunch at Giorgio's Saul and Abby headed to the Library of Congress. When they arrived, Abby asked to be excused for a moment and goes over to the counter to speak to someone. She pulls out her wallet, the gentleman smiled and leads them to a secure room.

"Hey what gives?" "How did you get us a private room?" "Not only private but secure actually." "How did you do that?" "I have my ways." Saul knowing Abby well enough knows better than to pursue the matter any further.

Meanwhile, at the office after reading the after action report the Colonel and the now more mollified General, are discussing what they think the next mission should be.

"Well Sir obviously you feel that they failed the last mission because not only were they unable to capture HG. They were not able to secure the plans either." "Well, that was their mission, capture HG get the plans, and they were unable to both, and they called for extraction earlier date." "May I remind you sir, that according to the after action report and them calling for extraction that they did what they had to do to preserve the STC. (*Space/Time Continuum*). "

"They still failed on both missions." "And I didn't bring either of them in because I wanted failure." "So, either we reign them both in, make stick to the mission, or we find other candidates for the job." The Colonel gently reminded the General that the primary mission was to maintain the STC and that they brought back invaluable intelligence. "And may I reiterate Sir that they followed absolutely the protocols you approve of." "If they had to extract themselves due to possibility of disrupting the STC they would call for recovery, that's protocol." "Also, they would have waisted valuable time, and HG would have even more opportunity to hide in the STC." "And we can't afford that, they have provided us with another opportunity to capture him and the machine."

"I suppose your right however failure is not an acceptable option." "When you fail a mission, you put lives in jeopardy." "General this is not war this is intelligence, and victory sometimes comes in different ways in the intelligence community."

"Colonel you're dismissed, You're giving me a headache and I don't want to hear any more."

The Colonel comes attention, salutes, does an about face and leaves the office. When he gets out of the office, he mumbles to himself. "Damn, stubborn old war horses." He returns to his desk and immediately fires off email to Abby

From the desk of: *Lieutenant Colonel Jack Spalding*

To: *AIC Abigail Thorne.*

Good news the General is calming down and beginning to understand your mission and reasoning. By Monday he should be in a better mood. Good thinking on taking the entire weekend off. Enjoy yourselves you've earned it.

Lieutenant Colonel Jack Spalding

A flash message comes across Abby's portable com desk. It's an email from the Colonel. "Apparently the General's calming his down, and according to the Email we can take the whole weekend we now have permission." "Not that we weren't going to do it anyway." "Well that damn General is beginning to piss me off." "Yes, he hired to do job, but neither of us are soldiers we're civilian contractors, so the Asshole better get that through his head."

"Well, we might as well come up with a "Battle Plan" to present to the General when we go back to work Monday." "Maybe that'll cool his jets a bit also."

Chapter 32

H.G. and Lissette head back to the Hostel. They spend a fortnight together, and H.G. tells Lissette that they should return back to Nice. "But what about the painting?" "Is it not proper that the model appear for all sittings?" "The Maestro told me it would not be necessary as he has completed the preliminary sketches. You will only be needed for the finalization and the touch up and the Maestro said he'd send dispatch when he's ready." "So why don't we return to our beautiful Nice and enjoy the comforts of home?" "Besides I've had enough of these barbarians, and I really wish to return to civilization" "I will depart from you in Nice, but of course return to you but I must, go back to Grenoble to take care of some personal business that needs attending to."

So H.G. and Lissette take the two weeks journey back home. When they arrive in Nice, he bids his farewell to Lissette and immediately departs for Grenoble.

Three weeks go by, and Lissette hears nothing from H.G. During this time however she discovers that she is pregnant with his child. She sends a dispatch to Grenoble and receives nothing back. A week goes by, and it is reported that the Count's body was found on the road between Nice and Grenoble. Devastated Lissette travels to Grenoble to inform the Gendarme that she was the Count's lover and that she was pregnant with his child. Being that the Count was dead, the court decides that she was to be made Contessa de Saintonge until after the birth of her child and her child comes of age, at which time he will resume the official title as heir to the Count. The Count was buried at **Cimetière des Saints-Innocents** (*Cemetery of the Innocents*).

Nine months later the Contessa gave birth to a male child. Between taking care of the responsibilities as Contessa and trying to take care of her child she had very little time to think of the painting that was made of her. Six months later her son, Phillippes died of Sudden Infant Death Syndrome. With the loss of her lover and the loss of her child the Contessa could no longer bear the pain and left her post as Contessa and joined a convent. While trying to redeem her soul, she began work tending the sick and ill during the black plague. 6 years later she succumbed to the plague and she herself died.

Leonardo upon hearing of the death of the Contessa and the Count decided to finish the portrait of the Mona Lisa in her honor and then 2 years after its completion he gifted the Portrait to Francis I, deciding that it indeed belonged where the Contessa called home, and it would remain in France for the next 500 years. The Mona Lisa was completed in 1519.

H.G. returned to Grenoble and promptly returned to where he hid the time machine. He set the Chronograph for the United States in 1994. He figured he'd hide there until such time as he could afford to go back into history and retrieve the plans. Too much time travel takes a burden on the traveler, so it would be better if he hides in an obscure era to recuperate.

He arrives in Berkeley California and sends the machine back to his time period and settles in Berkeley. He has the chronograph set to return to Berkeley in a few years in order for him to go back to the past and retrieve the documents. In the meantime, he sets up at the Phoebe A. Hearst Museum as the Department Head of the Renaissance Period.

When Saul's father was off on errands, he'd often leave his son in the hand of Dr. John Herbert (aka H.G.), who would take him around to the various displays and give him history lessons. His lessons intrigued Saul; they were so detailed at times that he would swear that Dr. Herbert was actually there when the events occurred. Little did he realize that indeed Dr. Herbert was there and had personally influenced many of the events that happened. Dr. Herbert made history fun for Saul which further enticed his becoming a historian himself.

Chapter 33

Friday afternoon General Thomas called Lieutenant Colonel Spalding into his office. "Colonel, I want Saul and Abby in my office by 0700 tomorrow. Send a com to Abby's desk tell them both to report back here." "Sir, we told them they were off until Monday." "I changed my mind. I want to get this mission completed successfully, this time." "The further we delay the better the chances we don't catch HG." "General, may I remind you..." "Remind me of what Colonel?" "Sir, they just got back from a long mission through time there needs to be time for them to decompress." "Soldiers don't decompress in combat; they don't stop until their mission is completed." "Sir, Saul and Abby are civilians." "Not under my command they are not they will be classified as soldiers." "Sir, you are also not considering that we are indeed travelling through time." "This gives us a bit of leeway we have pardon the pun" "All the time in the world to catch H.G." "Colonel, I don't care they are to report here tomorrow morning, they are to complete this mission, or I will find someone to replace them." "If they don't answer your email within 10 minutes, I want go get them and bring tell them personally to report." "Do I make myself clear?" "Yes Sir!" "But I still feel that they need the time off" "Bring them back here. End of argument" "Dismissed."

Colonel Spalding snaps to attention, salutes, does an about face and leaves the office. "Dammit, sometimes I wish I could just retire already." "I'm so sick of getting the brunt of his temper tantrums." "Now I have to go get those two and make them report to the General." "I wish that Son of a Bitch would make up his damn mind."

The Colonel sent an email to Abby's desk.

To the Desk of: *AIC Abigail Thorne and Professor Saul Millings*

From: *Lieutenant Colonel Jack Spalding.*

I really hate to have to do this. But your leave is cancelled the general wants you back in his office by 0700 tomorrow. I tried to extend your leave until Monday, but he insisted upon your return. If you do not respond to this Email, I am under orders to come pick you up personally.

Lieutenant Colonel Jack Spalding

Abby got a ping across her com desk. "Jesus H. Christ can't we catch a break?"

She called Saul and read him the Email. Saul is now pissed off. "This is utter BULLSHIT." "Personally, I want to tell the Colonel and General to shove the whole thing up their ass." "We sent them a copy of the after action, we sent them the new mission plan, what the fuck more do they want from us?"

Abby had never seen Saul become so agitated as to drop the F-Bomb. In a strange way she found it quite refreshing. "Wow!" "He does have a set of balls." "And here I thought he was just a mild mannered professor." "Abby, both of them be damned we're going to the Smithsonian tomorrow." "I made a promise to you that I would take you there and I'm a man of my word." "They can wait."

Abby sent back an Email to the Colonel.

To the desk of: *Lieutenant Colonel Jack Spalding.*

From: *AIC Abigail Thorne*

You might as well come get us then because as we said before, we are not reporting until

Monday. We are taking a well needed rest from that last mission, and we are going to enjoy ourselves over this weekend. It's bad enough you had us type out our after action report, and we also sent you a copy of our next mission plan. So, tell the General to get bent. We'll be back Monday. And if he doesn't like it, we may not be back at all.

AIC Abigail Thorne

The Colonel was left with no choice. He'd have to go to the hotel, and convince Saul and Abby to come in. Saul called Abby on the phone. "Hey Abby, sorry I got so gruff over the phone." "I'm just sick and tired of being demanded, when I volunteered my time and energy for this job." "Not a problem Saul, in fact it was quite refreshing." "So, anyway do you want to meet up in the hotel restaurant for dinner.?" Say around 8:30. That sounds good actually. I'll see you then."

Saul and Abby are coming down the elevator just as the Colonel enters the lobby of the hotel, he spots them as they get out of the elevator and calls out to them. "Saul, Abby, wait up a few seconds. I need to talk with you both." "We're going to get some dinner." "If you want to talk to us, you'll either have to wait until after we eat, or you will have to sit with us, your choice."

The Colonel agrees to sit down to the dinner. They order their drinks and meals and while waiting for their meals to arrive the Colonel tells them what the General said.

The General wants you back in his office tomorrow morning 0700 sharp." "He wants to discuss your after-action report and also wants to discuss your next mission plan." "Look Colonel! The after-action report spelled out exactly what happened and why we decided to scrap the mission." "When I made the rules up for time travel, I purposefully put in the caveats that if we felt that the mission would jeopardize the timeline in any way that we would call for extraction before an anomaly could take place. Thus, we did exactly that." "As I'm sure you read in our report, we were just protecting the timeline as it was what our job required above all else." "Yes, I understand exactly what and why you did what you did." "Then what the hell is the issue then." "The General is kind of a stubborn old war horse, and he thinks if a mission isn't completed that the mission, is a failure." "Well, not withstanding Colonel, we thought the same thing until we carefully analyzed the situation." "We both came to the conclusion that the mission though scrapped gained us some vital intelligence."

"I would tend to agree with you." "And on top of everything else our plans for our next mission are even more carefully thought out than our first mission was." "So, what seems to be the emergency here?" "We have plenty of time to work with and we should be able to accomplish the mission with relative ease." "I told the General the same thing." "However, he's got this old military attitude of *Hurry up and wait*." "Well colonel neither one of us is military therefore we both should be afforded the ability to think for ourselves and determine what the best course of action is going to be."

At this point their dinners arrived so they dropped the conversation. After eating their dinners and a bit of small talk, they told the Colonel that they would report at 0900 but because of their inconvenience He's buying dinner. The Colonel said, "Tell ya what come in at 0800 and I'll buy dinner tonight and tomorrow as well." "Or, I should say, the General will buy dinner because I'm putting this dinner and tomorrow nights on the General's expense account." "Our choice of location, right?" "Your choice of location for dinner." "Good, hey Abby how does Giorgio's sound to you." "That's expensive." "Yeah, but I'm sure the General makes enough money that he can cover it." Abby said, "Sounds really good to me." "So tomorrow night we'll do Giorgio's."

"As for tomorrow we're not going on another mission until I deem it's appropriate; And we are going to go to the Smithsonian. We are leaving no later than 10 o'clock. So, the General better make it quick."

Saul, Abby, and the Colonel depart company. Saul and Abby head back to their hotel rooms and the Colonel heads home. The Colonel is sincerely hoping that Abby and Saul arrive at 0800 but knows that the General isn't going to be too happy either because he wanted them in at 0700.

When the Colonel arrives home, he calls the General. "General I found Saul and Abby; they will be coming into your office at 0800 that's the earliest I could get them to agree to." "Colonel, I said I wanted them in at 0700." "I know sir, but may I remind you again they are civilians. And civilians don't take readily to being commanded." "Well, they aren't civilians when they are working for me." "Well sir you'll have to explain to them that."

Chapter 34

While Saul and Abby were at the Library of Congress, they had discussed the details of the next mission. Saul had decided he knew exactly when and where to find H.G. next. Saul, himself was enamored with Lissette when they were both in the Renaissance. When he realized that the Count was H.G. He figured that the H.G. and Lissette were lovers. So not only did H.G. hide the plans in the Mona Lisa, but also H.G. would want the Mona Lisa for himself as well. Saul had one more trick up his sleeve. He remembered the trackers that they had implanted in their arms and being that these trackers were the size of a microchip he could easily hide one in the Mona Lisa.

So, if he and Abby could get to the Mona Lisa before H.G. plant the chip, steal the plans they would be able to not only gain possession of the plans but also follow H.G. whenever he went. However, here was the rub. What if H.G. gets there first? Saul was banking on arriving in France, locating the painting, and getting it tagged before H.G. He figured H.G. would be hiding on a different timeline biding time and also planning his own escape. So, Saul says to Abby "We need to go back to WWII August 25, 1940, and recover the painting before H.G. does" "We'll take the plans from the painting replace them with a copy of the page which he stole which doesn't have the plans on them and place a micro tracker in the painting. We need to capture H.G. at his machine so we can recover both machines as well as him."

"That's probably the best and most well thought out plan so far." "H.G will think he got away." And we will be able to be one step ahead of him for a change" "And the Mona Lisa is the key."

"That's probably the best and most well thought out plan so far." "H.G will think he got away." And we will be able to be one step ahead of him for a change" "You should have joined the CIA." "You'd make a great James Bond." "Hell, I'm making this shit up on the fly actually."

Since their last mission, Abby was finding a newfound respect for Saul. Not only was he an excellent historian and able to make sure that history would stay the course; knowing exactly when they should refrain from further action, but also, he was capable of coming up with a really good course of action to take when it came down to the wire.

Saul in the meantime was finding himself respecting Abby's ability to teach him spy craft. She was a great thinker and was quick on her feet. She was definitely capable of maintaining her cover. She was able to follow a course of action necessary for the completion of her mission, and she understood the value of intelligence and surveillance.

The Colonel having read the after action report also was gaining a newfound respect for both of their talents. Abby and Saul were both excellent in the field. They maintained their covers well. They both were thoughtful and astute enough to know when the best opportunity was to scrap a mission that could otherwise have gone bad. The Colonel himself could have not chosen any better, two agents that could work together harmoniously. Hell, they almost seemed to think with one mind.

The General was not happy with the after action report because the mission was scrapped. He felt they could have stayed a bit longer to complete the mission. But the General's focus was not on the mission itself, it was on the final results. Those final results that he expected of the mission didn't come to pass, and therefore his two agents obviously couldn't complete the mission. If they failed, this mission how many more missions are they going to botch. He decided at that point to call Abby and Saul in early so that he could give them one final warning. If they failed again, he would find replacements for both of them. Soldiers that could complete the missions handed to them without questioning his orders.

Saul and Abby both woke up at 0600 got showered and changed into the clothes they were going to wear to go to the Smithsonian, called the Colonel to remind him that he had agreed to pick them both up, and headed downstairs for breakfast. While they were in the restaurant the Colonel arrived. He sat down at their table, and he also ordered himself some breakfast as well. He told Saul and Abby that breakfast was on the General. And proceeded to ask them, "Do you have your mission plan ready?" "As a matter of fact, Colonel we do." "Do me a favor, quit calling me Colonel here in public, call me Jack" "Okay not a problem." "Yeah,

I'm sick and tired of being addressed by my rank all the time." "I get it seven days a week and all I want is one person to actually call me by my given name." "So, what you got for me?" "Well Colonel, I mean Jack, this is the strategy we've come up with to catch H.G. We feel it's the best way we can do so and succeed in completing the entire mission." Saul laid out the plans to Jack and he approved. "Well, I can't see any flaws in this plan whatsoever and I think the Old Man will be pleased with this plan."

Chapter 35

Saul, Abby, and Jack arrive at the Pentagon at 0745 and head to the General's Office. When they get to the office the General is stewing. "I gave you orders to arrive at 0700 you are 55 minutes late." "Orders be damned General you're lucky we're even here at all." "We told you we'd have everything to you Monday morning, yet you insisted on us being here, ON SATURDAY! When we just got off a mission that took a lot out of both of us." "When we tell you the weekend is ours it's with good reason." "You don't give me orders." "I give the orders here." "Pardon me General, I'm not sure what capacity Abby is in, I do know that Colonel Spalding is under orders, however I PERSONALLY am a civilian contracted by you and volunteered to help you in this mission." "Thus, I can just as easily take and fly back to Berkeley, continue my tenure as a history professor and tell you to go piss in the wind." "And right now, I'm very tempted to do exactly that." "By the way try to find someone else with my credentials, good luck with that." "If Saul leaves, so do I." "I'll go back to the CIA and work back in the office again." Abby accidently spills the beans on her occupation because, she was so engrossed in the fact that Saul stood up for both of them. "So general, what do you intend to do now? Are you going to listen to us or are you going to continue to keep hounding us?" "You might as well tell us now." "So, we know whether or not to walk out of here." "And furthermore, the D.C. Sentinel would surely love to know what it is we are doing here."

"Okay. Okay, you've made your point. I'm just used to being in command, and if you can meet me halfway then we can continue to work together." "Well Sir, we have tried numerous times to meet you half-way as you so ask, but the meeting point must be mutual for this to be able to work" "Abby and I have developed a new mission plan and we're ready to submit it for approval. However, there are a few things I will need to get if we are to proceed with this mission. Which means I have to travel back to Berkeley. " "This means we are not going to be able to proceed with this new mission for at least two weeks. " The General read over the mission plan. "This sounds actually more feasible than your first mission plan." "General, my trip to Berkeley will give your team two weeks to develop the micro-tracker that I will need for this mission. It must be no larger than a microSD card so that I can place it without possibility of it being seen. It also cannot have any lights or sound as to alert of its presence. It must be non-descript in appearance and be virtually undetectable." "Also, it must be receivable by our holo-rings so you may want to reconfigure these rings for data tracking from the chip." "In the meantime, I am going to be in Berkeley." "Abby, would you like to come along, I'm going to fetch a few things, from my home and then I'm going to go visit my Maternal grandmother for a few." "It'll be a bit boring but better than doing nothing for two weeks." "Sure, I'll come along, it'll be a good change of pace."

"Are we dismissed Sir?" "Yes, you both are dismissed enjoy your two weeks but be back here no later than Friday 0900 hrs. so we can proceed with the mission." "That we can agree on General." We're heading to the Smithsonian, I promised Abby a tour. If you desperately need us shoot us an email."

Saul and Abby walk out. The Colonel is about to leave as well, and the general stops him.

"Jack wait a minute." "Sir?" "Take the two of them out for dinner on me tonight I want to make up for being such an ass." "I intended on it sir I told them in fact to get them here that you're buying dinner." "You did what?" "Get out of my office before I change my mind and take the weekend off yourself." "Jack, you realize you give me a headache right." "Dismissed". Jack calls out to Abby and Saul "Wait up may I join you?" "As long as you get out of that Monkey Suit, and there is no shop top for the rest of the weekend res" "I have a set of Civies in my office, I'll be ready in five in fact I'll drive us to the Smithsonian."

Jack quickly gets into his civies and they trio head for the Smithsonian. The car ride was a pleasant one. Jack told them that the General actually gave him the weekend off. So wherever in D.C. they want to go he can take them if they would like. "We'll be flying out Monday to Berkeley, so let's make the most of this weekend while we got it."

While they were driving to the Smithsonian, Abby was quiet. She was thinking to herself. "Man, I didn't know Saul had that big of a set." "He didn't back down once from the General." "I am starting to get feelings for him, but I just can't seem to get close to him, something just doesn't feel right." "Is it because we have to work together and working relationships, are doomed to failure?" "Or is it something more?" "Abigail don't ever get involved with a co-worker or a colleague especially in your line of work it can be detrimental to the mission and detrimental to both your safety as well.

The trio arrived at the Smithsonian, Jack parked the car ,and they headed inside. When they got inside Saul walked over to the curator's desk had a brief conversation with the Curator and they were given a grand tour even of some of the displays that weren't even open to the public. "How the hell did you do that?" "You've got your secrets Abby and so, do I?", Saul laughed. Jack surprised both Abby and Saul with a picnic lunch on the Smithsonian grounds. And then they finish up the day touring the rest of the museum.

While touring the museum Jack is thinking to himself "What a beautiful woman Abby, is strong, tough, self-sufficient, everything a man would ever want in a woman. Sadly, she seems enamored with Saul. So, I probably don't have a chance in hell."

"But you never know".

So, Jack drove Abby and Saul back to their hotel and then headed home to change for dinner. He only lived a few blocks away. Abby and Saul also ready themselves for dinner. Saul called in the dinner reservations. They went dinner around 8:00 pm. Because Saul and Abby had ordered dinner in Italian before, the waiter gave them menus in Italian. Jack looked over the menu and was totally confused. "What's the matter Jack?" "I can't read this menu, so I don't what to order." "Jack, do you have any meat preferences?" "I do like chicken". "Okay, well I have the perfect dish for you." "He'll have the Pollo al Marsala" (chicken marsala). "I'll have Linguine al sugo bianco di vongole" (linguini with white clam sauce). And Saul orders "marsala di vitello" (veal marsala).

"I know I promised I wouldn't talk shop, but the General messaged me when I got to my house and asked me to get, your itinerary so he can arrange a gulf stream to take you from Reagan International to Berkeley." "There'll be a car waiting for you in Berkeley, so you don't have to get a taxi to get to your conveyance." "I guess this the Generals way of apologizing".

"I'll send the General your itinerary and the General has arranged billeting in Andrews for you. So, you no longer have to stay at the hotel. " "So, after dinner you and Abby can pack your bags and I can drive you to Andrews on Sunday morning." "The General has also arranged IDs for both of you so you can get on and off bases without issue."

"What are the two of you doing Sunday Afternoon." "I don't know" "Well I'm going to take you both once we get you inside the base and to the house." "I'll take you to the Class 6, PX and commissary. " "So, we can get you set up.

While at the PX, Saul purchased a gas grill, some champagne at the class 6, and some nice filet mignon at the commissary." "The three decided they'd have barbecue." "They get back to the house and Saul fires up the grill and gets ready to begin cooking the steaks, Abby makes mimosas and Jack intercedes, "Let me do honors." Jack cooks up the steaks with the best seasoning and perfect temperatures. Saul made a nice salad, and some baked potatoes in the microwave." And they have a wonderful barbecue. That lasts throughout the day. After a nice cigar and a couple of brews Jack heads home. " Abby and Saul start to make the house a home. Though they both know they probably won't be living in it all that long because of the missions.

The next morning Saul and Abby get picked up by Jack and they go to the general's office pick up their itinerary and their boarding passes and then drive out to Reagan International where there is a Gulf Stream awaiting them. Saul and Abby board the Gulf Stream and head out to Berkeley.

When they arrive in Berkeley there is a car waiting for them at the airport and they drive to Stanford where jacks house is and pick up the papers that Jack needs. They spend the night and relax. Jack gave them a call to make sure that they arrived safely and that they were squared away. Saul told Jack that they were fine and that he would call Jack before they head back.

While at Saul's House, Saul began copying the drawing that was on the front side of the missing manuscript document. This was to be the fake that they were going to place in the hands of H.G. Also, he seasoned the paper with coffee as to give it a more authentic appearance. It was a very close facsimile to the original that Saul had seen in Leonardo's studio. In fact, it was so close as it would almost fool a collector into believing it was the genuine article.

Chapter 36

August 22, 1996, H. G. is working at the Phoebe A
Hearst Museum as the Renaissance Curator. He
remembered that he had a Baldovinetti sketch of
Lissette in his possession. He decided to put the
sketch on display with his Renaissance Art display
that he was setting up. The Note under the sketch
read "Sketch of an Anonymous Woman by
Alessandro Baldovinetti, student of Leonardo Da
Vinci."

On the 23rd approximately 100 people
showed up for the Opening Gala for the Renaissance
Art Show. This day was by invitation only to
museum patrons and donors. While perusing the art
several of them noticed the Baldovinetti sketch and
remarked that the sketch looked very much similar
to the Mona Lisa. So, they enquired as to where the
sketch came from and who was Alessandro
Baldovinetti. H.G. responded to them saying that
the sketch was an anonymous donor and the
research he had done on the sketch indicated that
Leonardo Da Vinci had a student named Alessandro.
"So, I am assuming that this Mr. Baldovinetti is that
student."

There was also paparazzi there and when they overheard some of the people enquiring, they began taking pictures of the Baldovinetti. It was the next day that the photo appeared in the Newspaper. Suddenly there was an onslaught of curiosity seekers coming to the Museum just to see the infamous Baldovinetti. H.G. decided that the best course of action was to close early and to take down the exhibits. He wished to preserve the integrity of the art pieces. And prevent damage, accidental or intentional.

Sunday afternoon he asked Jacob if he could take two weeks to go to France and view some of the other renaissance pieces for research purposes. Jacob granted him the time off. H.G. takes the sketch and goes to France to the Louvre to compare the sketch with the Mona Lisa. While on the plane he's thinking to himself , "So Leonardo actually completed the portrait, could that portrait really be the Mona Lisa.?"

When he arrived in Paris he checked into his hotel, picked up the tour guide, and began looking at the pictures of Mona Lisa in the guide and comparing them with his sketch. The pictures didn't clearly depict the same features but there were definitely some evident similarities. Similarities that were too close to be coincidental. But the only way he would for sure would be visit the Mona Lisa in person and see for himself.

The following morning, he heads for the Louvre. He uses his credentials as an assistant curator to get into the museum a little earlier than that crowd. He approached the Mona Lisa, held the sketch up next to it and began to compare the details. While he's doing this a crowd of people walk in and they observe a man with a sketch next to the Mona Lisa. Upon coming closer they realize the sketch looks a lot like the Mona Lisa and they ask him where he got the sketch and was it a Da Vinci? He replies. "I believe it to be from Da Vinci's time period and that it was done by a student.". "Do you have name for this student ?" someone enquires. H.G. responds "His name was Alessandro Baldovinetti".

The French press asked him if he would be willing to do an interview about the sketch, and what he knows about it. He obliged them and soon the word got out on an international level of the existence of the now famous Baldovinetti sketch.

H.G. left the museum but not without taking one final look at the Mona Lisa, as he was leaving, he turned toward her and mouthed the words. "I will return to you and take you back with me, my Lissette."

H.G. returned to the United States and continued his work at the museum doing all the research he could so that he would be able to return to the past, find Lissette, and bring her with him back to the future where they could live together happily ever after.

Chapter 37

Six months go by and H.G. is still unable to get away from the Museum. Until one day he receives a letter from Milan.

Dear Mr. Herbert

I've been following the art scene for some time, and I am a collector of Renaissance Art particularly the Da Vinci Period. Many of the master's got their start during that period and many a great painting of all genres was produced. When I read in the paper that you had found a Baldovinetti, I couldn't have been more ecstatic. You see sir part of my collection is from those of Alessandro Baldovinetti. In fact, I have seven of his paintings in my possession. If indeed your sketch is a Baldovinetti I would be willing to negotiate with you in regards to my own collection. You see sir I'm getting up there in age and I wish my collection to go somewhere it will be well taken care of. So, in order to discuss this further you will find enclosed in this letter a pre-paid ticket to Milan, as well as a prepaid hotel reservation and vehicle rental. Please Sir! Bring the sketch with you as I must see it for myself. For it is said it resembles the Mona Lisa. And if indeed that is so then my collection had definitely increased in its value. For If a student of Leonardo's had sketched the Mona Lisa, and indeed the Mona Lisa is the most famous of Leonardo's paintings, His student must have been present during that time period.

Sincerely

Pietro Giordano.

H.G. cries out with an exuberant yell. Jacob came running out of his office to see what the commotion was about. "You have to read this!" "It's incredible news". He hands Jacob the letter, Jacob lets out a whoop and the two begin dancing around arm in arm. After the initial excitement died down. H.G. asked Jacob if he could go to Milan. Jacob of course responded, "That's probably the dumbest question I've ever heard of course you can go." "See you in a week and by the way this is a paid trip so don't worry about your paycheck it will be reflected on it. Just bring back those paintings."

H.G. left for Milan, while on the plane he started to reminisce about the last time he was in Milan. How he and Lissette had spent many a night together in each other's arms. And he began to wonder what ever happened to her. He started to play the "WHAT IF" game with himself. It was then he decided he would definitely travel back into time to find her. Perhaps he could change their future. Or even their past. "Just to see my Lissette one more time." "I would do things differently."

When the plane landed at the Milan Linate International Airport, he stepped out of the terminal to be greeted by a 1938 Type 41 Bugatti Royale, with a chauffeur holding a sign with his name on it. He stepped up to the car and declared himself and the Chauffer opened the door and ushered him to take a seat. Across from him sat an elderly gentleman dressed in a fine suit who introduced himself as Pietro Giordano. They conversed awhile as they were driving to the manor house and Pietro asked to see the Baldovinetti Sketch. H.G. pulled it out of his briefcase and handed it to Pietro. Pietro after looking it over thoroughly said to H.G. , "It does indeed resemble the Mona Lisa as was so acclaimed." "The resemblance is in fact uncanny." "Truly the young lad must have been present and sketched her under the tutelage of Leonardo." 'I will

pay you $100, 000,000 US dollars for this sketch. "
Though the offer was very tempting to H.G. He
declined. "I am its protector, as it was donated to
the museum and on my honor Sir, I could not
possibly sell it. It is not my property. " " I
understand, and though I'm willing to pay for it I also
agreed that should I not be able to procure the
sketch that I would donate my paintings to your
museum." "Therefore, we shall go to my manor, and
you shall see for yourself the Baldovinettis' that I
have in my possession. Which at that time if you can
authenticate them, I shall plan with your museum to
take possession of same."

      When they arrived at the manor it was
indeed true that Pietro had possession of the
Baldovinettis'. H. G. Recognized these as the very
works that were on display in Leonardo's studio and
when he saw the painting of the still life, he knew
immediately it was indeed a Baldovinetti because he
was there when Alessandro was working on that
very painting. H.G. Authenticated all the paintings
and then called the museum. When Jacob
answered the phone, H.G. informed him that they
were indeed the missing Baldovinettis' and that he

was planning with il Signore Giordano to have them transferred to the museum for display and permanent safe keeping.

Pietro and Jacob made the proper arrangements for the paintings to be sent to the museum. Customs was informed and the package was to be flown in by private conveyance. When the Baldovinettis arrived, Jacob had them transported by special courier to the museum. After unpacking the paintings, they were each authenticated, named, carbon dated and labeled for display and a special display was set up for them. From hence forth they were to be put out on display on the date of the anniversary of their discovery and procurement. Four years later Dr. Herbert retired from the museum taking the original Baldovinetti Mona Lisa sketch with him. In the last days of his tenure at the museum he started to mentally deteriorate. He was known to spend hours talking to the sketch as if it were there with him and he called the sketch Lissette. A picture of him was put on display with the rest of the Baldovinettis' as their founder.

Chapter 38

While Saul was busy copying the manuscript, he told Abby to make herself at home. Abby toured Saul's house, noticing the whole time the cleanliness and orderliness, that was present. "That's odd, I've never seen a bachelor's house so well taken care or orderly." "He must have a cleaning service." "So, this is how the other half lives." She makes a pot of coffee, a couple of slices of bacon, and some eggs. While she's waiting for the coffee to brew, Saul steps out of his office. He sees Abby standing in the kitchen cooking over the stove. "What's that delicious smell?" "I decided to make us a quick breakfast and some coffee." "Well, it smells delicious, and I really could use the break."

After the breakfast, Saul and Abby sit down with their dossiers and plans for the next mission. They again go over the details carefully. And Saul shows her the copy of the manuscript. For Saul copying the manuscript was easy. According to the original letters which he retrieved and read; he could see that the plans for the time machine were done on the back of Saul's sketch of Lissette. It would be quite easy for him to re-sketch with a lot of accuracy that same sketch. He showed it to Abby and the picture of the manuscript that was present with the letters. She concurred that the similarities were there, and it could pass as the original.

Having finished finalizing everything Saul decided to call his grandmother and set up a meeting for lunch. "Hi Gram, I'm in town and wondered if you would like to join my colleague and I for some lunch at *"La Note"*. "Sure Saul, I'd love to have lunch with you and your colleague." "I can't drive like I used to so would you mind coming to get me." "Not at all we'll see you around 2:30."

They drive to pick up Gram, When they arrive at Gram's house Saul knocks on the door. Gram comes to the door and answers it. She spots Abby and immediately says, "Renee!" "That's impossible you're dead, wait a minute you must be Abigail. You look so much like your mother it's uncanny." "If I may ask, how do you know my name?" "Saul hasn't introduced me yet". "I think you both better come in and sit down." Gram gets them both a coffee and goes into the closet to get a photo album. She brings the album to Saul and Abby and opens it up to a wedding picture of Renee and

Jacob (Saul's father and mother.) Abby and Saul immediately notice the resemblance. And Gram tells them what happened.

"It's about time you learned the truth. I'm sorry it's been held from you both for so long, but it was hard on us all to actually be able to tell you what happened. Saul as you know your mother died at childbirth from TSS (Toxic Shock Syndrome) what you didn't know is that you were actually the second born and you were born postmortem via emergency C-Section. Abby that means you were born first. So, you are actually twins. " "Then why was I given up for adoption if I was the first born?" "Your dad was so grief stricken at the time because he dearly loved your mother, that he couldn't think clearly. He knew he couldn't handle a girl as he didn't know the first thing about raising one, and he also couldn't afford to take care of you both. So, he chose Saul and gave you up for adoption wanting you to have a loving and caring home"

"If that was the case, why did he name me then?" "He actually didn't name you Abby, the young nurse who was present at the time who put you in the incubator because you both have congenital defects, she named you Abigail. Jacob couldn't bear to give you a name because he knew that he couldn't be a father to you. " "I offered to take care of you, but I too was suffering because your mother was my daughter."

"Abby, Saul, Please I hope that you can forgive me for not coming to you sooner as I lost touch with Saul after your father died, and also I never knew where you were." "So please forgive me and let me be the family you have" Because we only have each other left.

"The only family that I have ever known were my adoptive Parents. After they died, I've be alone. I've never had a family to call my own until now. If you would be willing to accept me back into the family, where I first belonged."

"Of course, I will Abby I've always wanted a sister, and now I know I have one." "And I too, would be happy to be the grandmother that I should have been to you both."

"And Grams it's not that I'm doubting your story. But I would like to go to the Hospital where we were born so we can verify the facts and in addition get a proper birth certificate and such for Abby if truly what you say happened."

"Very well, we shall do that. I would not ask anything less of you both than to check to see if the story is true. Because for so long you've not known what had happened."

Saul, Abby, and Grams drove to the hospital in silence. When they arrived at the hospital, they asked to speak to the head of The Obstetrics Department. When they got to the third floor. The Head Nurse greeted them. "Abigail" Oh my goodness, you look so much like your mother God rest her soul." "How do you know my name?" "I'm the nurse who named you at birth." It was a very tragic birth, and I couldn't see you go without naming you. So, I named you after my own daughter." "I'm glad to see you turned out to be a fine and beautiful young lady." "Your parents would have been proud of you." "And I'm sure your adoptive parents are proud of you." "Actually, my adoptive parents are deceased. I've been on my own since I was 18." "I'm so sorry to hear that if I had only known." "So is there something we can do for you and Saul." Actually, yes can we have a

Mitochondrial DNA test done to prove our maternity and in addition if it should come back positive could we have a birth certificate made for both of us.?"
"Certainly, can do that, in fact we'll push the DNA test from the lab to be done within no later than two hours."
"All I'll need is a swab from both of you"

Two hours passed and the DNA test came back 99.999997 percent match with all thirteen markers present. The Hospital presented both with the birth certificates and record with Jacob and Renee's name as mother and father on them.

Abby, Saul, and Grams went down to the cafeteria and grabbed a cup of coffee it was a very emotional day, Abby and Saul excused themselves and went for a cigarette. "Saul, I thought you only smoked the occasional cigar." "Normally yes! But this situation is far from normal. Can you spare a cigarette?" "Sure". She gave Saul the cigarette and then lit her own. They stood in silence for a while smoking, and Saul said to Abby. "Thank you!" "For what?" "For being a part of my life, for being my sister, and for being my friend. I too was alone for a long time and I'm glad that we found each other." "I

Love You Abby", "I Love You Too Saul."

"And to think when we were back in the Renaissance, we were play acting as Brother and Sister not knowing that it was truly the case." "I'm finally believing there is no such thing as coincidences."

Saul, Abby, and Gram go to lunch. This would be the first lunch they would eat together as a newfound family. And this new but old family had a great time. Abby learned a lot about Saul and Saul learned a lot about Abby. They shared everything about how they grew up what their expectations were, what their dreams were, and what they had in common, which they found they had a lot in common.

They drop Gram at her house and head back to Saul's place. On the way Saul asked Abby if she'd like to see the museum that he virtually grew up in. Abby said, "I'd be delighted" So they drove the short distance to the museum. When they pulled into the parking lot, they spotted the marquee. It read "Baldovinetti exhibit". "Who the hell is Baldovinetti". Abby gave him a sideways glance and a punch to the shoulder. "Some little known student of Leonardo Da' Vinci's" "Oh wait that's, Nah it can't be my work." They both entered the museum to see the display there were 7 of the 8 pieces he had done sitting on easels." He recognized them all as his especially the Tern's on the shoreline and the Still life which Leonardo made him do to teach him shadowing. Also on display was a picture of H.G. with the caption below it saying in honor of the man that procured the collection Dr. John Herbert.

After realizing H.G. was his teacher when he was a child Saul recovered himself and he and Abby went over to the curator and inquired as to the status of Dr. Herbert. The curator informed them that Dr. Herbert retired several years ago and took the Mona Lisa sketch with him. He seemingly had a bit of dementia as he would often talk to the sketch as if it were a real person and he called it his Lissette.

Abby and Saul thanked the curator and promptly made their departure. They realized that they get back to D.C. and command because they had just missed H.G. by 4 years. And they could not delay the mission any longer.

Chapter 39

Saul called Gram and he asked her if she would like to come to D.C. with him and Abby for a couple of weeks. He explained to Gram that they had to cut their stay in Berkeley short because they were needed by their job a bit earlier than expected. Gram said, "I'd love to, that would be nice to see where you both are working, plus I've always wanted to go to the Nation's Capital." I'll call you soon we will probably be leaving early Monday morning so I'm going to pick you up Sunday night and you can stay here at the house with us." "So, pack a couple of weeks' worth of clothes."

Saul then called Jack. "Hey Jack, we're gonna have to fly back earlier than we anticipated we have to change plans we discovered a very hot lead on H.G. and we're going to pursue it. So, if you can arrange a Gulf for us. We also will have a third passenger with us, we will explain when we get there." "Well, the earliest flight I can get you is at 0500 Monday morning would that suffice, we'll send a car from Travis, and we will have the flight out of Travis ready for you." "Sounds good."

Sunday night Saul drove to his grandmother's house. Abby stayed back at the house cooking dinner for them all when they got back. When Saul arrived, grandma was ready to go and after loading the car with the luggage, she called Saul inside. She handed Saul a necklace which she said had been in the family for over 500 years and she wished for Saul to give it to Abby because it was normally passed down from Eldest female to Eldest female.

Saul placed the necklace in his pocket and drove them back to the house. They all ate dinner and relaxed then retired for the evening because they had an early flight to catch in the morning. Saul completely forgot about the necklace.

Sunday morning came and the car arrived for the trio. They loaded up the car and headed for Travis AFB not much of a word was spoken during the trip the trip took only 20 minutes. When they arrived at the gate the driver cleared them all and headed toward the flightline where a gulf stream awaited them. They boarded the gulf and took the four hour flight to Reagan International.

When they landed at Reagan international, they got off the plane. Jack was waiting down the other end of the runway about 400 yards away. They were about to head toward the car and Saul was nudged by Grams. "Aren't you forgetting something?" "Oh yeah." Saul reached into his pocket pulled out the necklace beckoned Abby to him and placed the necklace around her neck. Abby gave Saul a hug and a kiss in gratitude. Jack observing from a distance rushed up.

"What was that? You can't do that, you're …."

"Brother and Sister, we know."

Jack was flustered at this point. Jack had read their medical records and while reviewing their records had discovered that they were a DNA match.

They got into the car and drove back to the housing. The Four of them enjoying the trip back to the billets and of course, Grams was introduced to Jack. Gram liked Jack on first sight and could kind of see that Jack had a crush on Abby. Grams thought to herself "He wouldn't be a bad catch for her." "She ought to go for it." "Maybe while I'm here I could hook them up."

While they were in the car Saul noticed something different about Jacks uniform. He realized that Jack had gotten his colonel's rank and was a full bird, Colonel. "Hey Jack, Congrats man you've finally made full bird." "Yeah, finally after a long tenure waiting for my rank to raise." "Well, we will have to help you celebrate with another barbecue." "Sounds great. I'll even let you make the steaks this time."

After everyone unpacked and got settled in, Gram was properly introduced to Jack, and Saul and Abby told Jack how they discovered they were brother and sister. Jack told them how he made the discovery as well. And the confusion was settled. Jack went up to Abby while she was preparing the Mimosas . "Abby I was wondering would you perhaps consider going out with me on a date?" "Sorry Jack but I really have to decline the offer. You see I don't date people I work with because of the jobs we do can be life threatening. " "But I really am flattered by your asking." "If circumstances were different, I would probably consider it ."

Saul, Abby, and Grams sat down together at the kitchen table. Gram enquired as to what Saul and

Abby did for the government that they got such preferential treatment. Saul and Abby both said that due to the nature of their assignments they could not tell her the work they do only that indeed they worked for the government in the capacity of civilian contractors. No more explanation was needed after that.

Then they went over Abigail's history with her adoptive parents, how she traveled what her parents did for a living and how she grew up. Grams was pleased that Abigail ended up with a supportive family , and sad for Abby as well when she explained what had happened to them in Cairo.

Saul then arranged with Jack to be able to provide a ride to all the places in D.C. for Grams to visit while they were to be gone on assignments. This let them perform their mission without letting their grandmother know where they were going.

Chapter 40

Monday morning Saul and Abby went to the General's office. "There's a change in the plan General." "I realize we were going to go to France during World War II, but we, while in Berkeley, made a huge discovery. " "H.G. was actually here in the United States in 1994. Working at the same museum where my father was the curator." "We also discovered that he had the original sketch of Lisette with him when he retired from the museum and again disappeared. " "On the back of this sketch was the plans for the time machine. " "What we do not know is whether this sketch was the one that we were going to plant in World War II or if he had beaten us to the sketch." "So, we are anticipating that he will be returning to Renaissance to find Lisette. If we can arrive back there before he does, we can probably catch him in the process and save us from having to recover the sketch to determine if it's the original or not. "

The General was relatively pleased that they had returned earlier than expected. However, he did not want to have to change plans in mid-stream. Saul reminded him that "by planting the sketch we could be interfering with the timeline anyway and maybe he would have to have the original plans." "So, if we can recover the plans or leave them in place and hope that he built the machine based off of his future memory of the machine the plans would be totally unnecessary." The General was confused. "Are you saying to me that we don't get the plans we just try to get H.G., and we will get the plans from him. And the Mona Lisa still has the plans in it?" "Not necessarily General" "It means he could have still recovered the plans from World War II, and if that was the case we can still proceed with the next course." "But if we can capture him in the Renaissance, it will afford us the opportunity to kill two birds with one stone. We will have H.G. and the time machine." "If we don't capture him at least we will have more intelligence as to figure out accurately when and where he will be so we can." "It's a win either way."

"I have to trust your judgement this time Saul." "While you were away the Colonel reminded me not only of how important you are to the mission but also how necessary it is to have as much intelligence as possible." "Time travel is not as simple as it first seemed to be." "And maintaining the timeline is the most necessary thing to do, and so far, as I can see, you and Abby are the only two capable of doing just that." "I personally am confused by some of these concepts, so I am going to rely this time on your judgment. I have been able to get the trackers rigged up while you were gone. So, if you can plant them earlier, you'll be able to trace him then." "So, when do you expect to leave to the Renaissance again.?" "Well give us till tomorrow, Sir." "We will report back here 0800 and proceed with the mission."

Tuesday morning 0700 Saul, Grams, and Abby have a quick breakfast. "Why do you both get up so early for work?" "Back in our day it would be to milk cows and feed the chickens, but you both live in the city and you're up at the crack of dawn." "Because Grams, when you work for the Government especially a military branch, they keep ungodly hours." "Well, you both need to get more rest." "Maybe I'll tell Jack that you can't come in anymore until after 10:00." "You do that Grams, but sorry we have to grab our coffees and our bags and head to work." "We'll see you probably in about 1 to 2 weeks hopefully. In the meantime, enjoy the city and the sights. Jack has arranged everything for you." "Well then call me when you arrive at your destination." "We can't grams, but we will call you as soon as we are able to."

Saul and Abby arrive at the Pentagon and go immediately to the Lab. Everything is prepared for them; they change into their period dress and quickly consult with the General. "General, we will be landing the craft right outside of Saintonge, France. We know that's where the count was originally from, and we can trace Lissette's history as Contessa from there. If we arrive early enough, we can probably even catch up to Lissette before H.G. does and be able to lay in wait." "We will send the machine back to the Lab." "When we call for an extraction, we will let you know exactly where to send the machine and when."

"That sounds good." "We'll be waiting for your signal." "Your rings have been reconfigured." "They will now be able to track those trackers which you have without a problem." "To activate the trackers all you do is press the center of them, they will begin recording immediately. So, handle them carefully until you put them in place." The General hands Saul and Abby both about 4 trackers. They were as suggested no bigger than a microSD and totally non-descript. They could be easily hidden.

Chapter 41

March 6, 1513, it is only a week after the death of Pope Julius and the upcoming elections of the new Pope have the towns throughout Christian Europe abuzz with excitement. This was the perfect time for H.G. to land in to search for his beloved Lisette. He landed his machine in the forests surrounding Saintonge and headed into the town. He was dressed as a French Diocesan priest, and he called himself Pere Francis. When he entered the town, he reported himself to the local diocese as a visiting priest awaiting the annunciation of the Pope. And he went about the town seeking the residence of the Count de Saintonge of whom he had heard of in the past and wished to connect with. After inquiring several times at different locations, he was then told where he could find the manor house. While Journeying toward the manor he stopped at a wayside inn for a bite to eat and a tankard of ale. When his server arrived at his table, he noticed a necklace around her neck. This necklace looked very much like the one he gave to Lisette before he left her in Nice. So, he questioned the young lady, whom had a very familiar look about her, as to where she came by such a beautiful necklace, and what the meaning of the pendant was.

The Young lady replied, "The Necklace was a gift given me by my sister the Contessa prior to her leaving for the Convent to serve the Lord our God." "And what was the name of the Contessa if I may inquire?" "Her name was Lissette". "A lovely name and I noticed you said was, by was do you mean she took another name, or has she passed?" "Sorrowfully, she has indeed passed, she passed a year ago." "My condolences upon the loss of such a great lady." "Why may I ask did she join the convent?" "Well, you see father she was made Contessa because of her relationship with the Count de Saintonge. She was courting him and became pregnant with his child." H.G. at this news suddenly turned a bit white. Thankfully the candles that were lighting the room didn't make it evident. "And where is that child now?" "The young lad Phillippes as he was so named died 6 months after his birth." "How very tragic this young lady your sister's life must have been." "Indeed, father it was tragic but also it was blessed when she joined the convent, she turned over the manor to the mother superior, turned over the necklace to me, and served the sick and poor, who suffered the plague until she herself succumbed to it." "She is buried under the chapel in the manor house." "I'm sure if you asked the Mother Superior, she would allow you to give a blessing over her." "Indeed, I shall because a young lady of her caliber who suffered much and gave to others is deserving the Kingdom of Heaven." "By the way what is your name if I may so ask So that I can also give a blessing upon your kind heart as well." "My name is Josette Auberee". "The pleasure is all mine to have met you, Josette."

H.G. left the company of Josette with an air of despondency. When he heard of the tragic story told him he couldn't bring himself to try to pursue it any further. He would indeed, visit the site of her enshrinement and would honor her, praying for her to be carried to the Kingdom of Heaven. His adoration of her made him foreswear never to pursue another relationship. Instead, he would remain loving her till the end of his time on earth.

H.G. went to the manor house where he was greeted by the Mother Superior. She told him of the tragic story of Sister Magdalena, the name that Lissette had taken on when she joined the convent. Upon hearing the story for the second time he wept openly. He made another vow that day and it would be one that in the future he would honor wholeheartedly. He would do everything in his power to make her a saint.

Eventually, with the influence of H.G. and the retelling and recording of his precious heroine's life story the Catholic Church would indeed eventually canonize her and recognize her as St. Magdalena, Matron Saint of Courtesans, and other marginalized persons.

H.G. went back to his time machine, not wishing to stay in the Renaissance much longer and travelled back to 1996 where he visited the Louvre again and began talking to the Mona Lisa. He told the painting that He would never forget her and that he would do everything in his power to make her a saint. People observing this man talking to the painting and weeping thought him a bit mad and the Gendarme escorted him out of the museum telling him if he returned, he would be arrested.

H.G. returned to the United States, and

again he disappeared. He would remain there until he would be eventually discovered.

Chapter 42

Grams called Jack to come take her to the grocer so she could put some food in the house. Jack arrived to pick her up and take her to the commissary. While they were on the way to the commissary Grams decided to bring up the fact that Jack seemed to like Abby. Jack said to her, "Indeed I do, but I've already asked her out and she politely declined because she will not date someone she works with." "Well, we'll just have to convince her then won't we." When they got back to the house Grams told Jack to get changed into some real clothes and come back to the house for some homemade lasagna. Jack said he would and went home to change.

When Jack arrived back at the house gram had the Lasagna in the oven, She poured a drink for herself, and Jack and they got to talking.

"So, Jack, tell me a little more about yourself." "Well, there's not much to tell." "Sure, there is. Like where are you originally from?" "Well, I was born in Augusta, Georgia, I was raised pretty much all over the world." "How old are you?" "I'm

39". "Have you ever been married?" "No ma'am I'm single, I'm married to my job and the US Airforce." "What made you decide to join the Airforce?" "Well, you see my father was a Marine and was always deployed so I had to live with my grandparents when I was younger. They more or less ignored me so I kind of got into trouble. My father not being able to be present decided that the best thing he could do was send me to Hargrave Military Academy. So, I basically became a soldier at the age of 13 I graduated from the Academy with honors and was made a second Lieutenant. So, I joined the Airforce and became a pilot." "So where is your father now if I may ask?" "My father died when I was 16, he was killed in Cairo at the embassy bombing. He was posthumously awarded a Medal of Honor." "So, after I graduated from the Academy, I immediately went into the Airforce Academy in Boulder Colorado." "What rank was your father?" "He was a Lieutenant Colonel" "Well like father like son, except you're now a full-bird colonel I believe that's what they call it." "Yes Ma'am". "Well Jack if I was thirty years younger Abby would have to stand in line. " "If you want you can be my adopted

grandson." "And you can call me grams as well."
"That would be my pleasure grams". "Well, I do
believe that dinner is now ready. Shall we have
some delicious lasagna?" "The quickest way to my
heart is through my stomach so I'm definitely
game.".

   The two ate a wonderful meal and spent
the rest of the evening chatting. The following day
Jack took some time off to show Grams the sights
and such. Grams informed Jack that she cannot stay
longer than the week because the Homeowner's
Association is very strict about the appearance of the
houses and particularly the well-manicured lawns
and she wants to make sure that the lawn is properly
mowed. So, Jack arranged for a Gulf Stream to take
both of them to Travis AFB and then a car from
Travis to drop her at her house. He then flew back
to Andrews. He had to report to the General the
next day, and it was back to the grind.

Chapter 43

August 25, 1506, Saul, and Abby arrive in Nice and immediately send the machine back to command. They maintain their previous cover story as Alessandro and Alessandra Baldovinetti. When then enter the city, they immediately begin inquiring as to where they can find Lissette. They check all the local inns and boarding houses. They discover that she had left Nice and went to Saintonge where she was named Contessa. So, they hire a carriage and travel west to Saintonge.

Claiming they were on official business for Maestro Leonardo Da Vinci they managed to secure the location of the Contessa's manor. They were afforded lodging by the Contessa's Seneschal, after which they were granted an audience by the Contessa. The following morning Lissette received them both in the great hall.

"Come, come. Sit with me my dear friends you must be hungered after just a long journey from Milan." She ordered the cook to bring forth a breakfast for each of them and they chatted over breakfast. Saul and Abby enquired as to the whereabouts of the Count. "Unfortunately, a lot has happened since we last were in each other's company." "When we returned to Nice the count had said to me that he had business in Grenoble to take care of and he left me with some Francs to sustain me until his return" "Alas, three weeks went by and I discovered that I was with his child". "I sent numerous dispatches as to inform him of my condition with no response. So, I travelled to Grenoble to enquire of him to discover that he had met his demise at the hands of rogues on his way back to Nice." Abby and Saul noticed the necklace that was around her neck. It was the exact same necklace that Saul had given Abby. "What a stunning necklace you are wearing". "A this was given me before he left for Grenoble." "It was discovered that it was made as a gift for me as a token of his commitment to wed me." "What is the meaning of the pendant?" "It is the royal seal of this house." "When it was confirmed that I was his intended, the house and title were then passed to me." "What of your child?" "Six months after his birth he succumbed to crib death." "I'm so sorry to hear of that." "Would you like to return to Milan with us and allow Maestro Leonardo to finish your portrait.?" "So sorry, I must decline. For you see without the count or my Son my portrait would be meaningless to me. I will recompense Maestro Leonardo for the remaining balance due him, but my grief will not allow for a portrait to be finished of me." "We perfectly well understand Milady for in your position which we could not imagine the pain, we too would decline." "What is it that you will do now that you are Contessa?" "I have decided to abdicate my position and I shall give the manor to the convent which I will take cloister in." "In fact, I feel that I must redeem myself before God and betroth myself to him only."

"But enough of this talk please it's depressing." "Instead let me call in my sister and we shall have a dance and a game of ball and enjoy each other's company as it's been long waited for." Lissette calls for her sister who soon joins them at the table. The resemblance of the two is uncanny, they are virtually identical in appearance, save for a birthmark. "I would like to introduce to you my sister Josette, she is my older sister and also my lady in waiting." "The pleasure indeed is ours to meet you Josette".

After a day of revelries, they all went to quarters for the evening. The following morning Lissette called for Court. When all members of the court were present and also Alessandro and Alessandra, she made an announcement. "I call all ye forth today to inform you of my decision to abdicate my position as Contessa. As my last official act as Contessa, I affirm the following rulings. My court shall maintain its course in position of managing the city of Saintonge. All the revenue of my court exceeding the amount required to run the manor will be transferred to the care of my Sister Josette. Whom will be henceforth the mistress of my house. The Manor house itself will be transferred to the Sisters of the Ascension. With whom I will be future in attendance with and will be serving God and the people of God until my last days upon earth. I bestow upon my Sister also the royal signet of the house of Saintonge. Which shall be passed forward after her departure to the eldest female child in the lineage. This is my decree, and it shall be followed as foresworn." "It has been my honor and pleasure to have served as your Contessa for as long as I have done so."

Having witnessed this and being part of the assemblage both Abby and Saul knew that they had no more reason to stay and excused themselves saying they had to return to Maestro Da Vinci and let him know. They sent dispatch to Leonardo informing him of the Abdication along with the remaining monies due him. And they called for an extraction. After the death of Lissette Leonardo did indeed finish the painting and the Contessa de Saintonge would remain forever in history honored.

Chapter 44

Back at the Command Center new developments were taking place. A third and fourth time machine were built each of them having new technology for tracking and return sequences. They could be sent back and forth without having to be reset in the laboratory. Each had their own Flux Signatures which could be traced and also tapped into allowing for the command center to recall any of them to the center by simply tapping onto the Flux signature and opening a time portal.

It was discovered however that operating more than two at any given time would create rifts that would tend to cause the machines to malfunction and often wind up in places where they weren't set to land. So, the lab decided the best course of action was operating one machine at a time. They recently discovered, however, a second signature that was running slightly parallel to the one that was created by their machine.

They reported this phenomenon to the General. They were told to monitor the second flux carefully and see when and where the signature stops and goes. If this signature didn't belong to their machine it had to belong to one other person, the only other person who had a machine and knew about time travel and that was H.G. If they could tap into his flux, then perhaps they could redirect his machine to come to the lab.

Saul and Abby return to command. They go up to the General's office. "We missed him again apparently, we were mistaken, and he didn't return to the time we thought he was going to. However, we believe we may have a way to finally catch him. " "I've heard that before." "What do you propose this time?" "Well Sir, we gathered intelligence as to the fact that he was at the museum in Berkeley in 1996 and that he put together the display of the Baldovinetti paintings." "According to the Curator every year they put them on display. And every 10 years they hold a gala. If we go back to 2010 Berkeley, they are likely to have him as a guest speaker." "We can then catch him there."

"You better be right about it this time. I'm sick of all the wild goose chases." "General I'm sure of it." "Fine however this time I'm sending Colonel Spalding with you." "More boots on the ground."

"Remember this is a capture or kill mission. If you for any reason cannot capture him, you are to kill him understood." "We cannot let that slippery son of a bitch get past us again." "Fail this mission and I will guarantee you there will not be any other missions for you, in fact you both may find yourself nonextant."

The General dismissed Saul and Abby and then called Jack into his office. "Colonel, I want you to actually get with Saul and Abby before this next mission. They will fill you in on the details. You are going on the next mission with them." "But Sir I've never traveled in time." "Well, this time you will do exactly that. Don't worry it's only going back to 2010 not that far back and you're not leaving the United States." "Saul will explain the details to you." "This mission is to proceed in 3 days." "Why am I going?" "Because someone has to keep an eye on the both of them." "They've already failed two missions we can't have a third failure." "If for any reason they cannot complete this mission you are to complete it yourself and then you are to also remove them from the timeline." "Do I make myself clear Colonel." "Yes Sir." "Good, you are dismissed."

Jack met up with Saul and Abby and informed them both of what the General had said to him. They decided not to discuss the matter any further until they were in private. And all three headed back to Saul's quarters. When they got back to Saul's house, they immediately did a sweep for bugs, not a one saying anything to the other until such time as every room was cleared. Once they determined there were no listening devices in the room, they also turned off their rings and placed them outside, under the door mat. Then they went back inside poured a couple of drinks and discussed what the general had told each of them. Each were under separate orders. And they were told should one fail the others were to proceed with the mission and then eliminate the ones that failed. So, they all decided the best course of action.

Chapter 45

"The General is sending me on this mission to ensure that you complete your mission." "At least that's what he told me." "He also stated that if you fail this mission, I'm to carry it out to the end which includes, if I have to kill all three of you." "Of course, I don't want to do that and I sure as hell do not want to complete this mission either." "It's about time we find out what the hell that man is trying to do and put a stop to it once and for all." "I'm getting so sick of being the fall guy for his bullshit." "That's like the Al Hazreed incident." "If I had known that was a civilian hospital, I would have turned that damn drone around and sent it after the General instead for ordering the drone strike." "I wonder what the fuck else he's hiding." "So, I think it's high time we find out."

Jack was pissed, he's not going to obey an order which dictates to him to kill his friends just because of the whim of a maniacal, megalomaniacal General who is virtually trying to kill three birds with one stone. Ever since the discovery of the papers , the creation of the time machine, and the development of the Time Corp, It's been seemingly one disaster after another, and it seems to all lead back to General Lancaster Thomas. Being the General's Aid however has its advantages. Jack controls the General's calendar, and he happens to have a meeting with the Joint Chiefs at Camp David which will take about 2 weeks. This will give the trio enough time to run an investigation, get to H.G. warn him and still get back to command and put a stop to this hunt once and for all.

Another fortunate advantage that the trio had was the General was more or less entirely hands-off, when it came to the actual missions and time travel, he'd place the order only after the mission plan was drawn up and then he'd retire to this office and let the operatives run the mission. So, he would spend little or no time in the lab.

Saul came up with a plan to warn H.G. Indeed, they would all three go to the 2010 Baldovinetti Anniversary Gala, they would confront H.G. there and then they would allow for his escape under the agreement that he maintain a given cover and also that he works in the shadows for them. This would be the agreement reached. Also, they would then proceed to 2008 in both machines and find out exactly what happened with the Embassy bombing as well as what the General's connection was with Al Hazreed.

Abby volunteered to use her CIA contacts in the present as well as in 2008 and 2010 to follow up on the investigation of Al Hazreed. She would procure the documents and intelligence gathered on Al Hazreed as well as the complete dossier on General Thomas. Including the Non-Redacted reports. They would then compare all the intelligence gathered and confront the General.

Jack and Abby would be armed, and they told Saul for his safety he needed to be armed also. Saul hated guns. He would much rather fight with words or fisticuffs than use a gun. But Jack and Abby insisted. So, they bought Saul a Glock 43 which is a ultra-compact Glock .380 which can be easily concealed. And holds 6 in the magazine and one in the chamber. Saul reluctantly agreed to carry it hoping not to have to use it. Abby's sidearm was a Heckler Koch ported .45 with a 1911 frame, and Jack carried the M1911A1. .45 Automatic. All three hoped they would not have to use any of them.

After a long discussion the three sat down to dinner in silence each thinking about the mission and carefully considering what they would do. This would be their final mission under the General hopefully, and they would be able to do this mission carefully as to secure everything they needed to take down the General. Each had their individual motives for wanting to put an end to the mission. Saul knew that they couldn't kill H.G. because it would affect him and Abby, and it would create the time paradox which everyone knows can be detrimental, even if they killed him in the future, and they were around to do it. They were still unsure of the fact of killing an ancestor.

Abby wanted answers to her foster parent's deaths. And the General had prevented her from getting those answers. So, it's high time she was able to get them. And Jack also wanted answers to his father's death as well as he discovered from Abby the Embassy bombing was directly connected to Al Hazreed and somehow directly connected to the General. They would get their answers soon enough.

Chapter 46

The trio head out of the restaurant. Abby uses one of her disposable IDs to pay the tab and they call Hertz for a rental under Abby's assumed name. Once the rental arrives, they stop at the ATM and withdraw twelve hundred dollars. They go to a hotel pay cash and rent a single room. They sweep the room for bugs and begin planning out their course of action. Now knowing that the General is basically wanting to eliminate Saul, Abby and H.G. they are all going to have to do something about it. They are going to have to find H.G. not to capture him but to warn him and then ally themselves to him.

When Saul and Abby previously arrived at the museum, and they had discovered the Baldovinettis they talked to the museum curator. They of course enquired about the founding, and they were informed that Dr. John Herbert had found them and recovered them. They were also told that every year and every 10th anniversary after the millennium a special gala event occurs. This first event Dr. Herbert was the guest speaker. This would be their chance to get to H.G.

Saul formulates the plan to present to the General, this plan would include going back to that event capturing H.G. and bringing him and his time machine back to the present. This would be their ideal opportunity. Of course, they weren't going to follow the plan as this time things were going to be quite different. They would intentionally fail the mission, they would allow H.G. to escape and then of course claim that they are chasing him.

Jack would return to command tell them that they did find H.G. however due to circumstances they weren't able to make the capture they are in pursuit and awaiting the return of the Machine so they can find him. Jack will then return to 2010 and the trio will make their way to 2008.

Once their course of action was determined Saul, Abby and Jack parted ways and began their operation. Jack sent the General an Email across from his com desk.

From the Desk of: *Colonel Jack Spalding*

To: *Brigadier General Lancaster Thomas.*

Enclosed you will find a copy of our action plan for the final capture of H.G. This plan has been carefully thought out as to the details due to the fact we will only be traveling a little more than a decade backwards to initiate this plan. We will need about a week to acquire the necessary materials once we arrive, so we are going to travel back one week prior to the actual event. This is to ensure that we can establish the necessary credentials to attend the Gala as well as to ensure that we do not run into ourselves on that particular timeline. Careful planning and consideration have been put into this. We will also return to command after gathering a few more materials in our own timeline necessary for its completion. So, the operation will commence at 0900 one week from tomorrow. This hopefully will be our final mission pursuant to this particular issue. We will report to command when we are ready to proceed.

I know we have readied a few other machines we would prefer to travel together on this one so one of the larger machines which can carry three or more passengers will be necessary. This will give the laboratory enough time to calibrate and *ready the machine for this mission as well.*

Colonel Jack Spalding.

To the Desk of : *Colone Jack Spalding*

From: *Brigadier General Lancaster Thomas.*

Message received and plan acceptable. Everything will be readied here for your return. Let's make this the last time we have to find and pursue H.G. and let's get this mission done correctly. I'm sick of failures and this mission needs to be completed so that we don't have to compromise our own timeline.

Brigadier General Lancaster Thomas.

Chapter 47

Saul and Abby boarded the train to Chicago. Abby set them up in one of the CIA safe houses and then went to the field office to talk with her director.

"Abigail it's been a while since I've seen you how are you doing?" "Been very busy with this new assignment" "I've managed to get some time off so I'm in need of a few things if you wouldn't mind providing them for me." "What do you need?" "Well, I've decided since it's my time off I would follow up on my investigation of the Al Hazreed connection to the Cairo Bombing." "So, I'll need the reports from my previous investigation also the reports from the Cairo bombing and of course the final reports from the Al Hazreed kill order. " "I'm also going to need access to the embassy building." "So, I will need 3 sets of FBI creds, one female for me and 2 mail creds for my colleagues who will be helping me on this mission." "I'll need blank sheets for the picture and information cards. I will add the photos and information myself as to make sure the descriptions are accurate." "I'll also need blank passports with same." "I'll be deputizing two agents to work with me. They have already been vetted and I have worked with them both in my current missions so I can trust these individuals one hundred percent." "Can this be arranged?" "

"Well Abigail that's kind of a tall order." "But I trust your judgement and I'm sure you have valid reasons for all of this." "Plus, I'm curious myself as to what happened with the Al Hazreed and Cairo affair. So, I'll tell you what, I'm going to go ahead and get this set up for you." "As well as get you all the reports we have. You want me to send them to your normal drop.?" "No sir. I'll give you the location send one agent to the plane which I will have readied, and I will meet him there." "That agent must be directed to travel multiple locations before arriving, to make sure we don't have any tails."

"Make sure the vehicle is non-descript, and un-traceable." "I realize we are not supposed to be operating on U.S. soil, but the nature of this investigation requires that we do so with absolute discretion." "Remember when I said that I think the whole thing stinks with the Al Hazreed incident. Well, I think I have a hot lead that definitely smells as a coverup, and I know the parties involved are still trying to keep it that way." "If my gut is right, I'll not only expose the coverup but also I'll be able to apprehend the individuals involved." "And this goes all the way to the White House."

"Holy Shit! Abigail what have you gotten yourself into." "A situation which is going to require me to go in deep So once you get me the information, We will not be in contact until I resolve the mission." "Unfortunately, Sir I cannot tell you any more than what I have told you." "Well, is there an agent you can trust to deliver the information and paperwork you require?" "I can think of one and that's Matthews, he was trained by me, and I think he could handle this op without being caught." "Trust me Sir, if this mission wasn't so important I myself would probably not want to do it."

"I also want to keep it strictly under my jurisdiction." "No other agency is to know about the mission." "I know I'm asking a lot Sir. But I also know that you trust my judgement and instincts so I'm asking that you trust me now as well." "I do trust you Abigail and after this mission I do want the details in a report." "Feel free to redact any information which may compromise the identities of the other individuals." "And also, anything that may compromise your current mission status." "Again, I don't want to know about it.".

"Thank you, Sir, and I'll be expecting those documents in two days. I will be in touch as to where the drop will take place as I want to secure the area entirely."

Chapter 48

Jack returned to his office in the Pentagon. He punched up his com desk and immediately sent out the requisition forms for the documents concerning the 2008 bombing of the Embassy in Cairo, as well as the official reports of the Al-Hazreed take down. Using his S-1 clearance he was able to get un-redacted reports from the Cairo bombing. He then researched Al-Hazreed where he not only saw a connection between him and Al-Qaeda but also with the Mujahidin and the opium trade. "So, this is how they are funneling their money and such."

Jack was still looking for a connection which tied in the General. The only thing he could find thus far what that both the bombing of the embassy and the Al-Hazreed incident the General had given the order to direct a strike on the target. It was according to the report assumed that the Embassy had already been overrun and that there was no other choice but to strike it.

The next thing Jack pulled was the JSOC reports and footage from both missions. He saved them both to .mp4 formats and the JSOC reports themselves into .pdf formats. He then recovered the General's DD201 and his financial and medical histories. He was looking for anything that would indicate why the General is so keen on keeping things off of him.

In order to gather all this information Jack accessed the mainframe with his laptop, he then used a Keylogger to log into the system with someone else's security clearance. He then transferred the files to a thumb drive, wiped the cache from the server logs and then wiped the cache from his system as well. This way if anyone was to back track the actual login, they would find that someone logged into the system at such time and nothing more, and there would be no trace of him logging in.

After gathering the needed intel, he then went on with his day like any other given day. This would give him a cover and alibi story should he need it. He would then go to lunch, drop the thumb drive at a pre-arranged drop location which Abby would set up and then go back to work. Abby went over the procedure with him and even showed him exactly how to do the hack, where the drop would be and what the signal would be to leave when the drop was complete. Then it would be up to her.

Jack was very nervous about doing this part of the operation he had never ever done anything like this before and it would be the first, and hopefully the last time he would have to do this. He began to gain an even more intense respect for Abby and her training and skills. And he was also beginning to understand why she wouldn't date anyone she worked with unless the mission parameters called for it to maintain a cover story. He realized that her job required that she operate in ways than no standard person could ever possibly imagine.

But strangely enough he also found it exhilarating. The rush of adrenaline just from stealing from the Pentagon and getting away from it was kind of addicting. Abby also warned him of this phenomenon as well. She informed him that as exciting as it was, and scary as it would be, he would have to afterwards maintain a calm demeanor about himself. As if nothing had happened.   You must always maintain your natural persona regardless of how excited you may feel.

Chapter 49

Saul and Abby were waiting to taxi out from Midway Airport. They weren't going to taxi until Matthew's arrived with the documents. At which point they would fly back to DC. Pick up Jack and head to Berkeley . Abby would stop at the drop and pick up the thumb drive, call Jack's office and then they would take a train out of DC all the way to Berkeley. They figured the train would be the safest and most secure route to travel. Plus, it would give them three days to sort through their intel.

Once in Berkeley they would then let Saul gather whatever intel he had and also secure the documents until they could return. They would then call for a machine and head to 2010. The newer machines could travel forward and change locations and drop and within 20 minutes time after they left. They could be sent from the lab at command un-manned, and pre-calibrated. Jack would call command and have the machine dropped right in Saul's back yard.

Agent Matthew's arrived at the plane. Abby stepped off the plane and met him across the way. She took the documents from the agent and then reboarded the plane and after the agent left, they taxied and took off to DC. When they arrived in DC. Abby went to the drop location, called Jack, and told jack to meet them at the Train station in 1 hr. Jack went to the station entered the mall and waited for them to arrive.

Jack sat at a table in Kelly's Cajun Grille and waited for their arrival. He was extremely apprehensive. This current mission had too many variables and he wasn't sure if the logistics would meet the criteria to successfully pull it off. He arranged for the General to be out of his office for at least two weeks. This cleared him up to be able to travel with Saul and Abby, when and wherever they would go. Even though the General had already given him the order, he knew that the General was often prone to changing his mind last minute. So not having him there was probably the best route they could go.

Jack was never one to disobey an order from a superior officer. But an order to kill his friends, weighed heavily on his shoulders. He did not consider this order a lawful one. In fact, he felt the General had gone way too far in ordering him to do that. "What was the General actually hiding?" "By killing Saul and Abby as well as H.G. what was he trying to accomplish?" "How could their existence be a detriment to the timeline?" All these questions ran through Jack's head. He didn't know the answers but was sure anxious to find out.

Saul and Abby arrive at the Grille on schedule. They met up with Jack and the trio had lunch while waiting for the train. Abby had already procured their train tickets. They would take a sleeper car so they would have the privacy of not being disturbed by other passengers. While in the car they would go over the materials carefully and start correlating their notes. After finishing their lunch in virtual silence. They waited at gate 5 for their final departure. Each was carrying a small suitcase and briefcases. They would have no luggage that would be checked as to secure everything with them. Abby informed Jack that she had recovered the thumb drive and had it in her case. In order to bypass security, they each carried FBI creds that enabled them to be left virtually alone by security and they were able to pass through even carrying their sidearms. Abby spent the night before making sure that the creds were ready, and their passports were also set.

They recovered more money from several other cards at the ATMs under their assumed identities. Everything from this point would have to be done using cash. The tickets for the train were made with a cash purchase on a will call. Abby had prearranged everything while she was in Chicago. Neither Jack nor Saul questioned Abby as to how she acquired the necessary materials. They both decided this was strictly need to know and that they did not need to know.

Chapter 50

The trio boarded the train and headed out to Berkeley while in the car Abby took the thumb drive and pulled up the general's service record.

⇒ *7 June 1989 — Lackland AFB — Basic Training Security Forces — Cadet*

⇒ *7 December 1989 — Lackland AFB — Advanced Individual training — Cadet*

⇒ *9 June 1990 — Lackland AFB — Security Forces Officer — 2nd Lieutenant*

⇒ *8 August 1992 — Bagram Airfield Afghanistan — Security Forces Officer — 2nd Lieutenant*

⇒ *12 November 1994 — Dover AFB — Mortuary Services — 1st Lieutenant*

⇒ *19 July 1996 — Shindand AFB Afghanistan — Mortuary Services — Captain*

⇒ *17 April 2001 — Shindand AFB Afghanistan — Mortuary Services — Major*

⇒ *19 October 2007 — Andrews AFB — J.S.O.C. —*

Lieutenant Colonel

⇒ *23 May 2013 — Andrews AFB — J.S.O.C. — Colonel*

⇒ *24 August 2022—Current — Pentagon — Brigadier General*

The General's Service Record indicated that he went from Security Forces into Mortuary Services which begged the question; "why would an officer go from a combat role in Afghanistan to a non-combat role?" The only thing any of them could think of was that he had to have sustained some sort of injury and was taken out of a field command. So, the next thing they did was check his service record against his hospital records.

The hospital records showed that he sustained a gunshot wound to his right leg while at Bagram, He was transferred to Dover after a stint in Walter Reed and given a position in Mortuary Services. The treatment for his injury consisted of physical therapy and pain management medication. Which did not allow him to return to a combat role for some time.

When he returned to combat role it was as a Logistics Coordinator for J.S.O.C. and eventually an Operations Supervisor. Which meant he coordinated special forces operations for the U.S. Military and was able to initiate air strikes on particular targets.

Upon further examination they noted that he had received a special commendation for uncovering a smuggling operation out of Afghanistan. Apparently, someone is Supply was falsifying shipping documents in order to ship out large amounts of cash, and weapons to the United states illegally. The General had uncovered this operation and reported to his superiors his findings.

The Trio noticed from several of the reports and some of Abby's investigation on Al-Hazreed that smuggling of drugs was also occurring particularly that of heroin and it was being done through Mortuary Services, around about the same time that the general was serving in that capacity.

Adding up the intelligence they pieced together the tie in between the General and Al-Hazreed. That was the reason that he wanted

Hazreed dead. If Hazreed was captured, he could have blown the whistle on the whole operation. Which meant the General would have lost his rank and his career.

But they still couldn't piece together the reasoning behind the embassy attack. It would be by going back to 2008 they would be able to finally piece together the rest of the puzzle.

Chapter 51

Saul, Abby, and Jack arrive at Saul's house. Saul immediately calls people in his department to begin research on the 2008 bombing of the embassy. Abby swept the house for any listening devices. Jack waited for the all clear before he settled himself in. It was cleared. The three then started planning their mission for themselves. The general was given the false mission plan, so for all he knew they were going to proceed with the mission as written.

Saul's people gathered newspaper articles and news footage and discover several pictures of the embassy and determine that the damage to the embassy was significant enough to close it down but not to raze it to the ground. They noted however, that there was a missing piece to the satellite feed on the news reports. It was like ten minute segment had just disappeared. The video picked up a trail of a missile in the last few seconds of the feed, after the cutoff, before the explosion took place.

Saul, Abby, and Jack knew that they had to get to H.G. They had to warn him and also get him to cooperate with them in order to resolve the matter once and for all. So, Jack called for the machine and the trio headed for 2010. Saul knew that in 2010 he would not be at his house for a period of at least one month because he was out on a dig in Tenochtitlan Mexico. This would be the ideal time to drop the machine recall it to the command and be able to attend the gala.

Once they arrived in 2010 Saul called up the museum and requested three tickets to the Baldovinetti Gala. They were sent to his house overnight and the trio drove to the gala together. They enter the main hall, they were met by the curator, and they inquired about Dr. John Herbert. "Dr Herbert should be arriving shortly as he is the founder of the Baldovinettis and the keynote speaker."

"Can we have the opportunity to meet with him after the showing?" "Certainly, I can arrange it." "That would be wonderful, I'm a huge fan of Baldovinetti's work." "It is rumored that there was or is a sketch of the original Mona Lisa. That is something I would really love to see." "Is it on display?" "Unfortunately, no, you see Dr. Herbert refuses to put that sketch on display because he said it's the pride of his collection." "He's even been known to call it 'His Lisette'".

"Well, I still look forward to the rest of the collection it's been quite a few years since I was last here, and I'm sure there are a lot more interesting exhibits to see." "My company and I will be exploring the museum until the keynote address." "It's been a real pleasure to have met you." "The pleasure is indeed mine." "It's not often we have such esteemed guests at the museum such as yourself." "I will most likely be leaving a comfortable donation to the museum." "I do hope that you will consider it enough." "Just having you present is enough of a donation to the museum." "Your reputation as a historian and such is so valuable an asset to our museum." "I do hope we can get you to come lecture in the future also." "I would be honored to do that and will be in contact with you as to when it will be possible."

Saul, Abby, and Jack wander around the museum for about an hour. Dr. Herbert shows up to give his keynote address on the founding and anniversary of the Baldovinetti paintings. He does an excellent job of describing the history of the paintings, almost as if he were there when they were painted. Which of course he was. Saul recalls the many lessons he received as a child from Dr. Herbert and how accurate the descriptions of history were, and now as a result of his investigation he understands why Dr. Herbert was indeed so accurate. He knows he was there.

Chapter 52

The curator approached Dr. Herbert after his speech. "Dr. Herbert I have someone I'd really like you to meet he is a contributor to the museum and is much interested in meeting you and discussing the Baldovinettis" "Certainly, you may introduce me to this gentleman." The curator walked Dr. Herbert up to the trio. "Dr. Herbert, I'd like you to meet Saul Millings and company". "Saul Millings, my god I haven't heard that name for a long time, you must have been 10 the last time I saw you." "You are correct Dr. Herbert." "It's a pleasure to see you again Saul, and who are your companions?" "I'd like to introduce you to Miss Abigail Thorne, my sister, and Mr. Jack Spalding my friend and colleague." "The pleasure is all mine." "Is there a chance we can meet somewhere in private where we can discuss the Baldovinetti paintings further." "Well, if the curator will allow, we can always use my old office here in the building." "Would that be, okay?" "Certainly, It'll be fine, and I will make sure you are not disturbed."

The four enter the office together. Dr. Herbert suddenly glances over at Abby and seen that she had the necklace on. "Where did you get that necklace?" "It was passed down to me from my grandmother who was supposed to give it to our mother before she died being that it was supposed to go to the oldest daughter." Trying to maintain his identity H.G. said, "I've seen that necklace on the Baldovinetti sketch of the Mona Lisa." "I know grandfather considering the fact that Lisette gave it to her sister Josette at the time of her abdication." "Mr. Well's I of course know who you are because Saul and I have been following you through time trying to catch up with you." "You see it was discovered that you are the great grandfather of Saul and I." "Saul found your letters and a time machine was built." "I knew I recognized you and Saul, but I thought I only recognized Saul via my being his tutor." "Indeed, you should have recognized us, we are the Baldovinettis, or I should say were."

"Well, you definitely caught up with me, I really don't know how you both managed so well." "It's in our blood. Mr. Wells." "Well, you might as well call me grandfather considering that we are related by blood." "Fair Enough." "Now that you've caught up with me what is the intention of the chase to begin with, perhaps we can clear it up or let it be?" "Well grandfather, the person we work for is a General in the United States Air Force." He's basically sent us to capture you and the time machine so that you can't interfere with the current timeline." "However, we have decided that after the General put a kill order on you as well as apparently on Saul and me, that we would not initiate a capture but rather a warning to you." "Saul what is your position on this matter." "I'm with Abby, we cannot afford to take the chance of causing a temporal paradox." "So, we have decided to warn you of the reasons behind the chase and ask you to work with us to help us take down the General." "And Jack's involvement?" "Jack is the Generals Aide and our friend." "When he was asked to secure the success of this mission, he was told to take out all three of us."

"Wow!" "So, what do you propose to do?" "Well, we are going to ask you to maintain your cover as Dr. Herbert." We are going to go to 2008, we're sending Jack forward to 2024 to tell the General that we are in pursuit of you. " "In the interim I think you made a promise lately." "Yes, we seen the newspaper article about you're almost arrest in Paris at the Louvre. " "Indeed, Lissette was canonized she was Canonized on February 14, 1969, we are going to let you go to witness her canonization and keep your promise to her." "We know how much you both loved each other."

"We're going to meet up in 2008 Cairo, Egypt and then once we gather the intel, we need from there we will return to 2024 on September 11th at 1300 which is 1 pm so we want you to set the coordinates on your machine for that date and time once you get done in 1969 to arrive at the pentagon in the general's office lobby these are the exact coordinates. 38.8719° N, 77.0563° W and it's room 33 floor 3. Once your machine arrives, we will lock onto your time Flux and move your machine into the lab. So, dismount your machine immediately." "By then we will be in the General's office confronting him." "Please make sure your arrival is prompt."

"We will arrest the General and then you will be free to go about your own business. Under the condition however that you don't alter the timeline   in any manner." "Or, if you want you can stay as Dr. Herbert and work with us." "The choice is yours on that."

"Are we in agreement as to the plan?" "Yes, I think this is an excellent plan and will go smashingly well." "Jolly good then and it's really a pleasure to have the chance to meet my actual descendants and family."   "It's funny how your mother and father completed the circle, you and your father whom I worked for, who are related to me, and your mother being related to Lissette." "Time is indeed a strange mistress."

Chapter 53

The four head back to Saul's house. Final preparations were made, and Jack called for the machine to be sent to them. They all travel to 2008 Cairo. Jack takes the time machine to 2024. There he confronts the General. "Sir we were unable to capture H.G. due to the close proximity of civilians within the Gala, we weren't able to get him alone to capture or kill him. Saul and Abby are giving chase as he escaped to 2008. I immediately took the machine back here to inform you of the turn of events." "So again, another failed mission. I said that if this mission failed, I would have all of you finished. Get your ass back to 2008 find all three of them bring them here, I will dispose of them myself. And in addition, Lieutenant you can start preparing for your court martial for disobeying a direct order." "Now get the fuck out of my office."

Jack left the generals office and proceeded to wait in his office until after he knew the General had left for the day. He then went down to the arsenal prepared three cases for Abby, Saul, and himself. He placed within these cases maps of Cairo, a laptop, thumb drives, an explosive charge that was rigged to go off if anyone tampered with the security measures or locks, and a false bottom which held a Mach 10 with two 30 round magazines in case they should come under some severe fire while investigating in Cairo.

He drew up a set of orders to procure the time machine to travel back to 2008 to meet up with Saul and Abby at a predesignated location. He then boarded his time machine and headed back to 2008. When he arrived, he met up with Saul, Abby and H.G. and handed Saul and Abby their briefcases explaining to them what the procedure would be for them and how they operated. Then they let Dr. Herbert go and he left in his machine promising to return to 2024 within the week.

The trio then left to head to the embassy building. They presented their FBI credentials to the guard who let them in. Once they entered the building, they could see the extent of the damage caused by the explosion. But they also noticed other details. They noticed that there were gunshots all over the walls of the building, there was also various cameras strategically placed which of course would provide a valuable asset if they could recover the films and the recordings were all available from the time of the assault to the time of the explosion.

They would also search all the individual offices logging in all the evidence collected into their report from each office, designating a particular number and name, and taking photos prior to bagging materials. This was to ensure a proper forensic reconstruction of the events which would help them determine the cause and effect.

Since the bodies of the individuals who were killed were removed prior to their arrival they also needed to get ahold of Mortuary Services and locate the names and identities of all the victims. This would also provide them with a lead as to who was killed and by what and why.

Once they established the method, motive, and opportunity as well as the chain of events, they would then compile complete dossiers on all the victims and provide for the families of same a bit of closure as well as award any medals etc. that would be merited to the individuals who perished. Plus, they would research any medals and all service records both civilian and military of the victims to establish an adequate timeline of the events.

Not wanting to leave any stone unturned they made sure to collect all remaining documents, tapes, correspondences, books, files etc. from all the offices. This resulted in an inordinate amount of evidence which had to be collected and shipped to the safe house and then later to be sent to 2010 for analysis. So, the machine would have to be called to several locations prior to them returning to 2024.

They would return Jack first to 2010 where he would then send the machine back to 2008 the evidence would then be loaded and sent unmanned forward to Jack who would unload the evidence and send the machine back to pick up Saul and Abby. For all of them this would be a task that would take several days and have to be done carefully as not to arouse suspicion at Command who would be monitoring the transfers. So, they all decided their next best course of action would be to remove the tracking chips from their forearms and destroy them, they would manually set the machine back and forth and they would have to be very concise. They could not allow for any mistakes.

Chapter 54

With the proper coordination the team successfully moved all the materials to the safehouse where they began the long tedious process of sorting the evidence and piecing it all together. Indeed, there was an attack on the embassy by the Mujahideen however the attack consisted of predominantly small arms fire and could have been suppressed rather easily by a simple convoy of security forces being moved in and surrounding the area. The use of the tomahawk missile was unnecessary. The tomahawk had missed a direct hit on the building causing moderate structural damage and some internal damage. The injury to death count of persons in the building was approximately 38 dead and 195 wounded. However, many of the dead including that of the death of Abby's parents was not caused by the explosion. It was determined during autopsy that both had died from single gunshot wounds to the head.

A trajectory analysis indicated that these

wounds actually came from inside the building as opposed to sniper fire or small arms ricochets from the outside. Which meant that the wounds were made intentionally and potentially the tomahawk strike was used to attempt to cover up the real events. The official reports indicated that 29 of the deaths were from the partial collapse of the building and the remaining were from gunshot wounds. Which begged the question as to whether the shootings occurred after or before the actual strike took place.

Jack's father was killed in action while trying to rescue the ambassador. His death had resulted from a gunshot wound from outside the building which ricocheted off the wall and penetrated his chest killing both him and the ambassador. This was deemed a death from sniper fire as the round that was extracted came from a 7.62x54mmR shell fired from most likely a Mosin Nagant rifle the trajectory of the bullet indicated that it was fired from approximately 250 yards away and from a rooftop. This was definitely death by sniper fire. The obvious target was the ambassador.

Abby's parents upon further investigation

were killed by a .380 pistol round to the forehead, which was indicative of an execution style murder. Being that they were analysts the documents discovered in the office were reviewed very carefully by the team. It was determined that there was an investigation being run by the State Department on the possibility of a connection between the Al Qaeda, and a drug smuggling operation headed up by Al-Hazreed. Apparently, Al-Hazreed was filtering heroin through Mortuary Services and shipping the drugs out in the coffins of fallen soldiers to the U.S. The opium trade was highly active during this time period and the rise in Heroin and opiate usages in the US was on a rapid incline. The investigation was almost complete prior to the death of Abby's parents and there were never any official reports in the 2014 investigation because no documents were found.

Because of the oversight on the part of the team the documents went missing, official reports from the future did not indicate any connections whatsoever. Abby, Saul, and Jack could most likely correct that in the future because they had gathered all the evidence as FBI agents and had properly secured the evidence. Which would of course lead to a future investigation of the whole affair.

Because of this final investigation the team were able to determine that the Al-Hazreed take down of the Embassy as well as the future takedown of Al-Hazreed were both intentionally done to draw suspicion from the General because he was in charge of Mortuary Affairs at the time of the Embassy bombing and he had later upon failure to take down the building decided the best course of action would be to take out Al-Hazreed so that he couldn't blow the whistle on the whole operation.

The General had connected himself with a new supplier and was continuing the smuggling operations while even in JSOC. However, the new method of transport and the new suppliers were never actually determined, because the scale of the operations was a lot smaller and more dispersed and classified.

Chapter 55

With all the evidence gathered together from 2024, 2008, and 2010 the team was ready to confront the General. They had enough evidence to initiate an arrest and they returned to 2024 and contacted the OSI. After turning over all the evidence they had gathered they had enough evidence for an arrest warrant to be served. Abby using her CIA credentials and her status as a CIA Agent in charge requested from the OSI the jurisdiction and ability to serve the warrant and officiate the arrest. Due to the amount of evidence acquired by the team, permission was granted to her and the OSI turned over the Jurisdiction.

In the meantime, all the evidence was compiled into one group to be prepared for a congressional hearing. So, a joint task force headed up by the CIA was soon established. Their primary goal was to correlate the tons of evidence sort through it and put together a case to be put in front of the Senate Judiciary Committee. So, while all this was going on the team decided to confront the General serve the arrest warrant and finally put an end to the General's plans.

The team entered General Lancaster Thomas' office on Sept 11, 2024. Abby flashed her CIA Cred's at the secretary and told her to vacate the lobby and go elsewhere. She also showed the secretary the warrant so she knew that there would be no announcement. The warrant specifically stated that it was a no-knock warrant. So, it could be served without being announced. The secretary immediately complied. It was 1245 hours when they arrived.

They barged into the Lance's office and announced they had a warrant for his arrest. Lance accosted them. "Under what charges?" "We are placing you under arrest for the following charges." "Smuggling of controlled substances, conspiracy to commit murder, murder in the first degree, murder in the second degree, crimes against humanity, treason and sedition, and running a criminal enterprise." "This is bullshit. I have done nothing of the charges, and you can't prove shit." "General I have to advise you of your rights." "Under Article 31 section B of the Uniform Code of Military Justice. You have the right to remain silent, you also have the right to know the nature of the charges placed against you which I have informed you off. You have the right to procure an attorney during questioning, or you can by request receive the aid and assistance of the United States Judge Advocate General's Office. You are being detained pending a court-martial hearing and will be held for a period of no more than 72 hours during questioning. Do you understand the Article 31b rights as I have stated them to you, and do you wish at this time to waive any of these rights in question.?"

"No, I'm not going to waive any of these rights because I'm not going to be charged with Jack shit." "You can't arrest me!" "I'm a General in the United States Air Force." "This warrant states otherwise and we are indeed putting you under arrest Sir." The General pulled out his 45 and pointed it at Jack, Saul, and Abby. He was waving it around like a madman and ranting that he would kill them all if they came any closer to him. 1303 H.G. arrived in the Lobby. He sent the machine downstairs and then barged into the office because he was running late. When he entered the office the General started and pulled the trigger, shooting Jack in the shoulder. Jack dropped his gun and H.G.

Picked up the gun and fired it hitting the General in the same leg as he had injured in Afghanistan. "Son of a fucking bitch!" "The general dropped his gun the MP's having heard the two gunshots quickly rushed through the door they saw H.G. with the Gun in his hand and immediately ordered him to drop the weapon. H.G. released the magazine and then placed the gun on the ground in front of him. And raised his hands." "I want them arrested." "He shot me in the leg!" Abby ran over to Jack raised her badge and said, "Arrest the General, he shot this colonel." "I also have a warrant for his arrest which I was attempting to serve when he shot the colonel." "The person standing with his hands up actually saved our lives." "Who are you sir?" "I'm Dr. John Herbert I had an appointment to see the General but was running late." "When the General shot the colonel,

I just reacted." "I don't know what he's talking about I didn't have an appointment with him." "Besides that's not Dr. Herbert anyway it's H.G. Wells the creator of the time machine." "We have three of his time machines in the lab downstairs." "I'm the head of Time Corp." "I want all of them arrested." "We don't know what the general is talking about." "We are here to serve this warrant for his arrest for the Cairo bombing as well as the Al-Hazreed Hospital bombing. We've been investigating this for some time, with the cooperation of this Colonel." "So would you be so kind as to call in the medics to take the Colonel and General to Walter Reed and place the General into custody." They called the medics and escorted the General out in cuffs.

"I will get you all, No matter what time or place you go I will find you and you will all get what's coming to you." "You cannot hide from me." "You shot me in the same leg I got shot in before". "You Mr. Well's will pay for that."

Epilogue

After Jack recovered from his injury, he was given an accommodation for the capture of the General and promoted to Brigadier General and placed in charge of the Science and Research Division. Abigail decided it was high time to retire and she went into the private sector as Jacks aide. Saul and H.G. continued to work for the Time Corp helping to solve glitches in history as they came up.

The General was placed in the stockade pending his Court Martial Hearing. He was committed to the psychiatric ward for a period of 72 hours, then placed in protective custody. But he wouldn't be in there very long. There would be retribution for his arrest and court martial he would get revenge on them all.

Made in the USA
Middletown, DE
11 January 2023

21211866R00144